Joanna looked at Lord Tony Ashford across the ballroom. He was as breathtakingly handsome, flawlessly attired, and wonderfully graceful as ever. But now the cream of the *ton* shunned him—except for the ravenous beauties who had an appetite for a man of his scandalous reputation.

Her heart pounding, Joanna walked to where Tony stood in close conversation with the notorious Lady Cathcart. Though Joanna's dress was not cut quite as low as Lady Cathcart's, it nonetheless showed far more of her bosom than Tony had ever seen before as she held out her dance card and lamented her lack of a partner for the next waltz.

"You tricked me into that, Joanna," he growled into her ear as they moved off onto the floor.

"You were just going to dance with a few upper-class whores like Lady Cathcart, is that it?" Joanna challenged him.

Joanna saw Tony smile as his gaze flicked down to her neckline, and his arms tightened their grip . . . she realized she had entered a competition in which she had more at stake than she had ever dared dream of. . . .

SIGNET REGENCY ROMANCE
COMING IN JUNE 1994

Anne Barbour
Lord Glenraven's Return

Emma Lange
A Heart In Peril

Emily Hendrickson
The Scoundrel's Bride

AT YOUR LOCAL BOOKSTORE
OR ORDER DIRECTLY
FROM THE PUBLISHER
WITH VISA OR MASTERCARD
1-800-253-6476

Lord Ashford's Wager

Marjorie Farrell

A SIGNET BOOK

This one is for my aunts,
Mary, Joan and Connie Farrell.

SIGNET
Published by the Penguin Group
Penguin Books USA Inc., 375 Hudson Street, New York, New York 10014, U.S.A.
Penguin Books Ltd, 27 Wrights Lane, London W8 5TZ, England
Penguin Books Australia Ltd, Ringwood, Victoria, Australia
Penguin Books Canada Ltd, 10 Alcorn Avenue, Toronto, Ontario, Canada M4V 3B2
Penguin Books (N.Z.) Ltd, 182–190 Wairau Road, Auckland 10, New Zealand

Penguin Books Ltd, Registered Offices: Harmondsworth, Middlesex, England
First published by Signet, an imprint of Dutton Signet, a division of
Penguin Books USA Inc.
First Printing, May, 1994
10 9 8 7 6 5 4 3 2 1
Copyright © Marjorie Farrell, 1994
All rights reserved

 REGISTERED TRADEMARK—MARCA REGISTRADA

Printed in the United States of America
Without limiting the rights under copyright reserved above, no part of this publication may be reproduced, stored in or introduced into a retrieval system, or transmitted, in any form, or by any means (electronic, mechanical, photocopying, recording, or otherwise), without the prior written permission of both the copyright owner and the above publisher of this book.

BOOKS ARE AVAILABLE AT QUANTITY DISCOUNTS WHEN USED TO PROMOTE PRODUCTS OR SERVICES. FOR INFORMATION PLEASE WRITE TO PREMIUM MARKETING DIVISION, PENGUIN BOOKS USA INC., 375 HUDSON STREET, NEW YORK, NEW YORK 10014.

If you purchased this book without a cover you should be aware that this book is stolen property. It was reported as "unsold and destroyed" to the publisher and neither the author nor the publisher has received any payment for this "stripped book."

1

"Good evening, my Lord."

"Good evening, Jeremiah." Tony Varden, Lord Ashford, gave the man leaning over the half-door at 75 St. James Street one of his most charming smiles.

"Go right up, my lord, and good luck to you."

Tony bounded up one flight of stairs and waited for a moment on the top step as he was surveyed from the spy-hole in the second door. The retainer in charge of this door was always silent, and far from being the one-eyed giant the spy-hole brought to mind, he had to stand on tiptoes to peer out. But his vision was perfect and no one ever made it through who didn't belong.

One more door, and Tony was admitted into the inner sanctum, which was everything the antechambers were not. Brilliant chandeliers hung from the ceiling and fragrant shrubs lined the walls. Immaculately dressed waiters circulated unobtrusively, offering the finest brandies and clarets and guiding patrons to the supper room where refreshments rivaled those at the most fashionable soirees.

Lord Ashford headed straight for the altar of this temple, a large oblong table covered in green cloth. Some few of those standing around it greeted him quietly, but most were interested in the hands of the dealers rapidly laying down cards.

Black was first, as always. Ten, jack, five . . . eight. "Three," called the dealer. Then, without a second's pause, the red: six, ace, two, king, three . . . ten.

"Two," called the second croupier.

A collective slumping of shoulders on the black side of the table, a noticeable eagerness on the red side as the dealers raked in the house profit and distributed the winnings.

Lord Ashford gently pushed his way through to the black side, and drawing a few guineas out of his pocket, placed them on the table.

"Four," called the black dealer.

"Two again on the red."

No change on Lord Ashford's face, except for a fleeting smile at the waiter who offered him a whiskey and soda. He set the glass down in front of him on the edge of the table and fished out two more guineas, murmuring, "*Sur le noir*," as he placed them on the black oval painted on the table.

"Two."

"*Deux sur le noir*," murmured Lord Ashford with a short sigh of relief.

"One."

"*Un sur le rouge*," he whispered in the same even tone, without a flicker of disappointment on his face.

Another two guineas went down on the black.

"One."

"One *après*."

Merde, thought Lord Ashford.

This time, however, his luck had changed. On the deciding deal, it was thirty-three on the black, thirty-five on the red. And so his two guineas came back to him.

He stepped back from the table as a young man pushed his way through. It was James Colter, Viscount Lindsay, looking drunk and feverish. The next two deals were in favor of black and Tony quietly pocketed his guineas, watching young Lindsay out of the corner of his eye. The boy, for that was all he was, could not govern his emotions, and slapped the table in delight as he won. Then the deals began to go to the red. In the next two hours, Lord Ashford won and lost, won and lost, but the sums remained small. Not young Lindsay, however. He played a total of seven hundred guineas and lost it all. As the dealer raked back his last shillings, Lindsay stood there looking lost, reaching deep into his pockets for anything, anything to lay down. He was not cast down, Lord Ashford realized, because he had lost such a sum, but because he could not go on playing.

The boy finally stumbled backward, looking down at his watchless waist, his pinless cravat, his ringless hands. Tony was sure that had there been a business in little fingers, Lindsay would have sold his to get back in the game. As it was, he suddenly let out a laugh, turned, and pushing past patrons and waiters, ran down the stairs.

"A Johnny Newcome, Boniface?" Ashford asked the man next to him.

"Nah, 'e ain't no punter, but 'e be a regular patient of ours," replied the blackleg with a wink. "'E gets werry 'ighblooded at times, and for 'is own 'ealth, we got to fleabotomize 'im, as it were. 'Ow are you doing tonight, m'lord?"

"Not badly, Boniface. Keeping afloat."

"You might want to play the red for a while, my lord."

"I'll stick to the black," replied Tony, placing another guinea on the table. On the next five deals he won and played his winnings. He was just pocketing sixty guineas when he heard someone running up the stairs. The room became utterly silent as all eyes turned to the door, wondering if a constable had somehow gotten past the watchdogs. But it was just young Lindsay, a grin on his face, with his coat buttoned up to his cravat. He pushed into the crowd on the other side of the table and lay down eight shillings.

"There. On the red." And the red won. Not every time, but again and again, even on the *après* deals. When he had won back one hundred pounds, the boy looked up and unbuttoned his coat, exposing his naked, hairless chest.

"Went to a pawnbroker on Jermyn Street," he crowed. "Best thing I ever did." He lay down twenty pounds. "Here, waiter, champagne all around!"

Ashford shook his head. Lindsay might not be a Johnny Newcome, but he was acting like one. He, the Earl of Ashford, prided himself on not letting on to anyone, anyone, how he was faring. Oh, they knew. Of course they knew, the blacklegs and the dealers. But they would never know from his face, his laughter, his groans. That satisfaction he wouldn't give them.

It was five a.m. before he pocketed his money and went home. All in all it had been a good evening. He had come with twenty guineas and left with forty-two. And back in his room he had a leather drawstring bag with one hundred guineas, which was untouchable. He prided himself on that fact. His pockets were not to let, nor would he ever have to sell his shirt to play. And of course he had Ashford.

Ashford was the only reason he was spending his nights in gaming hells, he would tell himself. It was the need to save his inheritance and provide for his mother that drove him out, night after night.

Ashford was a moderate-size property in Kent. It had been in the hands of the Varden family from the time of Henry VIII, as had the earldom. And although the Vardens had never been fabulously wealthy, they had been comfortable for generations. Until the present earl's father, in an attempt to *become* fabulously wealthy, had almost impoverished the family. Having put his faith and his money into government bonds, he lost both when the rumors of Wallington's defeat at Waterloo started coming across the channel. He sold when the price was lowest and awoke the next morning to realize that if he had just held on for a day or two, he would indeed have tripled the family fortune. As it was, he was left as metaphorically shirtless as young Lindsay had been literally.

The earl suffered a stroke within two days and died without regaining consciousness. Lady Ashford walked around saying to anyone who would listen, "It was a blessing, really. He could not have borne being helpless," all the while tears running down her face at the sudden loss of her husband. Her younger son, Anthony, was a captain in Wellington's army and did not return home for the funeral. Indeed, he did not even hear of his father's death until his return in August.

Her older son, Edward, upon assuming the title, made it clear that he would spare no effort in restoring the estate. He closed the London town house, closeted himself with his manager and the family solicitor and presented his wife and mother with a detailed plan for economizing.

Neither woman resented it. In fact, both admired Ned for his seriousness and sense of responsibility. They only worried about him, for he physically exhausted himself during the day and stayed up late at night going over the accounts, trying to find more ways to strengthen their finances.

Captain Varden was transferred to the War Office staff in London, a virtual sinecure now that the war was over. He visited Kent on the holidays, but spent most of his time attending every social function to which he was invited. He did no more drinking and gaming than many of his contemporaries. Which was to say: a lot, but never to excess.

He admired his brother's sense of duty, but was grateful that he was the youngest. He had never envied Ned the earldom, unlike some younger sons. He knew he did not have the temperament for the responsibilities. On his occasional visits, he would look at his brother's drawn face and wonder what choices he would have made had he been handed such a burden.

"Why don't you sell, Ned?" he asked on one of his visits, after the women had gone to bed.

"Sell Ashford! It has been in the family for three hundred years. Of course I couldn't sell. I must preserve it for the heir, whether that be a son Charlotte and I have, or you."

"At the rate you are driving yourself, there will be no heir," said Tony, who was only half joking.

"No, no, you will see. One or two more years of this economizing and we will be on our way out of the woods."

But Ned did not have even one year. He caught a cold that March, but insisted on supervising the planting himself. The weather was raw that spring, and his cold quickly became an inflammation of the lungs. Within two weeks he was gone, and Captain Anthony Varden was the new Earl of Ashford.

It was too much for all of them. The countess collapsed in the churchyard and was confined to her room for months. Her daughter-in-law, who was very fond of Ned's mother, stayed on with them until she was sure that the dowager would recover. And a week after his brother's death Tony, trying to feel close to Ned, sat down at his brother's desk and rifled through the papers Ned had been working on. When he came to the last account entry, made in an obviously shaky hand, he could hold back his own grief no longer, and spent one night in hell, crying for "Ned, Ned," as he had when he was a boy and had fallen off his pony or gotten tangled in his own fishing line.

He left the next day, intending, as he told his mother, to speak with the family solicitor and become better acquainted with Ashford affairs. But one morning in old Farley's office convinced him that he was not meant to be an earl. Or at least not one cut out of the same cloth as his brother. Things seemed hopeless. He couldn't imagine how Ned had thought they'd begin to come about in two years. It seemed as if it would take twenty. Of course, crop rotation and small investments were not Tony Varden's forte. His talents were for leading men on the battlefield. His mind was made for military strategies, not financial tactics.

And so he began frequenting the hells. Oh, at first it was only to drop a few guineas, drink more than he should, and thereby keep his mind off his overwhelming burden. But gradually his play became deeper and his bank drafts larger and his losses more frequent.

He had made one decision: to lease the town house, which at least brought in some steady income. But instead of turning any of the money over to Ashford, he drew on it to fund his play.

He owed money all over town, for he kept up appearances. His valet had become quite expert at turning away his creditors. But it was only a matter of time before they caught up with him.

The one thing he had not done—yet—was to borrow against Ashford. He would have railed against anyone who suggested it. Ashford was not at all in jeopardy. He was doing all this to *save* it. He would never do anything to endanger his mother's security. But the estate seemed to hang around his neck like the ancient mariner's albatross. He couldn't, wouldn't, ever sell, for that would make Ned's death meaningless. But if only, somehow, he could be relieved of this heavy burden. . . .

2

"I am very worried about Tony Varden," said Lord Thomas Barrand, peering over his newspaper at his wife and daughter.

"Why is that, Father?" asked Lady Joanna.

"I had thought his frequenting the hells this past year merely a temporary reaction to Ned's death, but it has been months now. And word in the clubs is that he is badly dipped."

Joanna, who had been watching her old friend and neighbor for weeks and suspected that things were going badly, tried to keep her voice expressionless as she asked: "Do you think he is in any real danger?"

"If by that you mean losing Ashford, yes. For it seems it is almost all he has left."

"I am very glad that nothing ever came of your *tendre* for him, dear," said Lady Barrand to her daughter. "It would be a terrible thing to break off a betrothal, but that is what we would have had to do."

"There was never any chance of a betrothal anyway, Mother," replied Joanna lightly. "Tony only kindly paid his attentions to a former companion in mischief, and that was two years ago."

"Tony was never a bad lad," said Lord Barrand. "Just not cut out for the earldom. Such a shame Ned didn't live. Tony would never have gotten himself into such a coil otherwise, I am sure. He was always a lightweight compared to Ned, but he has a good heart underneath."

"I always thought Ned would have been the better match

for you, Joanna, had he not found Charlotte," said her mother. "But then, he would have died and left you a poor widow . . ."

"Oh, Mother!" Joanna looked over at Lady Barrand with affectionate exasperation. "Ned never gave a second thought to me, or I to him."

"I know, I know. But it is a shame. Your marriage to one of the Vardens would have made such sense."

"Now, Lydia, that is enough of that," said her husband. "Joanna has all of London to choose from. And Tony seems to have chosen elsewhere."

"Do you mean Lady Fairhaven, Thomas?" asked his wife. "That certainly would be one way Tony could come about. Fairhaven left her all his fortune, didn't he?"

"Yes. The estate and title went to his second cousin and the money to his widow."

"The new Lord Fairhaven is hardly poverty-struck, Father," commented Joanna. "After all, he managed his cousin's business for years."

"Yes, he has built up a tidy fortune of his own, I've heard."

"I wonder," mused Lady Barrand, "if Fairhaven set up his will like that for them to make a match someday."

"I had not thought of that, but you could be right," said her husband. "However, the way things are proceeding, the last earl must be disappointed, wherever he is! Lady Fairhaven has encouraged no one this Season but Tony Varden."

"But she is an older widow, Thomas."

"Only by a few years, my dear. And she is still as attractive as when she married Fairhaven."

"I never did understand how her parents could have done it. A seventeen-year-old girl married to a forty-six year old before her come-out! Some parents only see their children as pawns in a financial chess game!"

"But the marriage appeared to be a happy one, Lydia. She was a devoted wife to him and was genuinely grief-stricken when he died. If she thinks she would be happy with Tony, at least this time it is her choice."

Throughout the conversation, Joanna had kept her face free of expression. She did not want either of her parents to guess at the depth of her feelings for Tony.

She had had great hopes for her first Season, for like her parents, she too had thought a match with one of the Vardens would make great sense, but for entirely different reasons. Lord and Lady Barrand were thinking of how conveniently the estates marched together. She thought only of Tony.

They had all grown up together, she and Ned and Tony. They had ridden their ponies, fished and swum in the river, and played endless games of make-believe drawn from the legends of King Arthur. Even then Ned was the responsible one, likely to call them back from reckless climbs or keep Joanna from wading in too deeply when they went fishing. Tony, on the other hand, would dare her to follow him over a particularly high jump, and follow she would, hoping that if she could jump as high, or climb as well, he would notice her.

One of their games had ended in a never-to-be-forgotten disaster, told over Christmas punch for years after. Ned had been Sir Meliagrant, kidnapping Guinevere and tying her to a tree. Tony was Sir Lancelot and was to have been her rescuer. Unfortunately, Tony had been distracted by a deer breaking cover and had given chase after it, completely forgetting his role. Ned waited for an hour at the "crossroads" where they were to have their duel. When Tony never arrived, Ned assumed that he and Joanna had forgotten about him and he went home. It was several hours before the two boys arrived back home, neither accompanied by Joanna.

By the time they raced to the tree, Joanna had gone from boredom to fury to real fear. When she finally heard them shouting her name, she willed herself to stop crying like a silly baby and faced them with an "I could care less" face. Her hands were numb and her shoulders sore from pulling at her bonds, but her feet were well-shod and she bruised both their shins quite effectively. As Ned and Tony jumped back and incoherently tried to explain, Tony shamefacedly admitting that he had completely forgotten her, she couldn't decide whether she wanted to howl with heartbreak or laughter. She already knew she adored him. She could never have forgotten him. Her sense of humor won out. It was too much a Tony thing to have done. They all begun to laugh helplessly when she said: "Fortunate that I wasn't Guinevere at the stake, waiting for Lancelot. I'd be a pile of ash by now, wouldn't I?" she said after they'd untied her. Then, between giggles, she begged them both to leave immediately, before she disgraced herself. They looked blank for a moment, then blushed and got themselves out of sight so she could hike up her skirts and relieve herself.

When she rejoined them, they patted her awkwardly on the shoulder and called her a great gun and apologized all over again.

"I will just know better than to expect romance from you, Anthony Varden . . . Or you, Ned," she added hastily.

But she had. She had waited for Tony to see her as something other than Joanna the good sport and old friend. He never did. He went away to university and came home and danced with her at local assemblies and regaled her with stories of his exploits. She was the first to hear of his intention to buy a commission, but that confidence meant nothing more than that he regarded her, as he never tired of saying, as his oldest and best friend.

He was on the Continent for her first Season, which almost ruined it for her. She had so hoped that seeing her in town as a marriageable young lady would open his eyes to the fact that he had loved her all along. He was there for her second Season and faithfully partnered her and gossiped with her and teased her about her conquests. But he never held her close during a waltz, much less attempted a kiss.

She had offered her sympathy when his father died. She had flung herself into his arms and sobbed uncontrollably when Ned's coffin was lowered into the ground. A few days later she had penned him a letter, offering her deep sympathy and her own shoulder to cry on, should he ever need it. But he never spoke of Ned to her and had spent this, her third Season, hovering around Claudia Halesworth, Lady Fairhaven.

Lady Barrand was correct: Lady Fairhaven's parents had seen their pocket-Venus daughter as a meal-ticket. But although an undercurrent of gossip had featured Lord Fairhaven as a Bluebeard, the truth was that he had fallen passionately in love with his petite blonde neighbor almost immediately upon his return from many years in India. He had amassed a huge fortune in his twenty years away, and Claudia's parents decided that they had no problem with his money coming from trade since there was so much of it. Lord Fairhaven not only took their daughter off their hands but saved them the expense of a Season.

Society predicted that in a year, Justin Halesworth would be indifferent to his wife and that she would embark on an affair with a younger man. Society was wrong.

Claudia had gone through the courtship and ceremony in a kind of daze. Her parents had been telling her for years what her destiny was to be. She had accepted their control over her life and had never hesitated in either her response to Lord Fairhaven's proposal or in her recitation of her vows.

When they reached their new home, however, the reality hit her. She was a complete innocent yoked to a man thirty years her senior whom she hardly knew. She had stolen frightened glances at him in the coach. He was tall and spare with gray hair and weather-darkened skin. Her mother had briefly explained what would be expected of her that evening, but as she looked down at her husband's long-fingered hands, she began to shake at the thought of him touching her.

Lord Fairhaven noticed her shivering and placed his coat around her shoulders. When her shivering didn't stop, he took her hand in his and said: "You must be as frightened as I am, my dear."

Claudia took a ragged breath and looked up into his face.

"Oh, yes," he continued with a smile, "this is as terrifying for me as it is for you, Claudia. Here I am, a decrepit earl, hoping to make my young bride's wedding night a pleasurable experience, while she is worrying how she will hide her displeasure."

Claudia found her voice. "Surely not doddering, my lord," she said, with an attempt at humor.

"Justin, please, my dear."

"I am frightened . . . Justin. But more because I am so young and inexperienced than that you are old."

"You are as kind as you are beautiful, Claudia," Lord Fairhaven replied, with a twinkle in his eye. "But I promise you that one good thing about my having so many more years than you is that I also have, um, the experience. You are not to worry about your innocence, Claudia. It is what attracted me to you. Tonight I thought we might just dine privately and retire early and separately. We will make our way slowly."

Claudia's grateful look more than enough made up for his forbearance, thought Fairhaven. And so they had a comfortable supper together. He was a great storyteller and had many tales to tell about his years in the East. By the time he led Claudia up to her door she was more relaxed with him than she had ever thought possible.

When she awoke the next morning, she contemplated the door connecting their rooms for a long time. She *could* wait. He had made it clear that he would wait until she was ready. But why wait like a scared rabbit for something that was inevitable? So she drew on her silk wrapper and opened the door.

Her husband was awake and reading in bed. He looked at her in surprise as she stood on the threshold, and then patted the space beside him with his hand. She crawled under the covers, and he put his book and his spectacles on a bedside table.

"So you have come to brave the old lion in his den, eh?" Lord Fairhaven reached up his hand and gently smoothed her cheek. Claudia gave a slight shiver.

"Still frightened, my dear?"

"No, no. That felt . . . nice," she whispered.

Lord Fairhaven ran his finger down her cheek again, stopping at her mouth. "And this?" he asked, as he leaned over to kiss her.

"Yes," said Claudia with a smile after his gentle kiss.

Her husband slipped off her wrapper and his eyes gazed appreciatively at her small but ripe form. Claudia blushed, and before he could help her, shrugged herself awkwardly out of her night rail and lay flat, her arms by her sides.

"And now you think I am going to just fall on top of you and do it?" asked her husband, with that twinkle in his eye that she was beginning to appreciate.

"Aren't you? My mother said it would be quick . . . a little painful . . . but that I wouldn't suffer long."

"Oh, my dear," said Fairhaven, letting out a laughing groan. "I am amazed this island is populated at all! No, Claudia, one good thing about an older husband is that he will go more slowly and more pleasurably for you. Let me show you." And he proceeded to caress, gently and tenderly, every inch of her until her arms came up around his neck of their own accord and her legs around his hips without her even knowing how they got there. And after the slight pain, there was indeed great pleasure.

Their marriage was a very happy one, despite all the dire predictions. Claudia came to love her husband very much, although she never felt the passion for him that he so clearly did for her. When he died after a brief illness in the fifteenth year of their marriage, she was devastated. She had stayed by his side while he was dying, telling him how happy she had been during their years together.

"And you do not regret marrying an old man, then?" he had asked one afternoon.

"I do," she replied, "but only because I want more years with you."

"And my only regret is that I could not give them to you. And that we had no child."

"You have given me all I could ever want, Justin," she whispered, tears slipping down her cheeks. She wasn't telling the whole truth, for she *had* longed for a child, although she had kept her great disappointment to herself.

"No, but I have given you all I could, my dearest. After I die, I want you to find someone your own age who will show you that there is even more than we had."

Claudia was sobbing quietly by then. "Please, Justin. I can't bear it. I cannot imagine wanting anyone else. I mean to live out my years as your widow."

Justin patted her hand. "All right, we will talk of this no more. But you will remember this: that I wish for your happiness. I don't want you to bury yourself in Devon."

"I don't think I will stay here with Mark, Justin," said Claudia.

A spasm of pain passed over her husband's face, but he ignored her concern and said: "Mark will inherit the title and Fairhaven, but I have taken good care of you, Claudia. You will have my fortune. You need never be dependent upon anyone. I have made sure of that."

He had also made sure that his cousin, who had visited them often over the years, would have a good reason to seek her out. And what could be better than to have his line continued by his cousin and his beloved wife?

3

Claudia had returned to her parents' home almost immediately after her husband's funeral. She had kept only two secrets from her husband during their married life: one, the depths of her distress over their childlessness, and two, her dislike of his cousin and heir.

Mark Halesworth was only a year older than his cousin's bride and he made a trip to Fairhaven the summer after the marriage. He was a good-looking young man, and although their acquaintance was recent, the earl and he got along very well. At first, Mark was merely polite to his new relative and Claudia suspected that he disapproved of her, perhaps believed that she had only married the earl for his fortune. As the years went by, however, and it became clear that there would likely be no children, Mark became friendlier. She was so young and naive when she married that it took her all that time to realize that the coldness she felt had little to do with Mark's concern for Justin's happiness and all to do with his possible displacement as his cousin's heir.

Lord Fairhaven had offered to support Mark in the study of law, but Mark begged instead for a position in his cousin's business. Mark had worked his way up, until, by the time of his cousin's death, he was the manager of Halesworth Ltd.

Although, according to gossip, he had had several mistresses, his passion was clearly for finance, not for women. Claudia, who had always felt him to be a cold man, was convinced that his sorrow at his cousin's death was all surface. She was especially suspicious of his relief that she had been left well off.

"For no one could have been a more devoted wife, Claudia. You deserve to be rewarded," he told her after the will was read.

Claudia, who was still in shock from her loss, hardly took his words in, but later, when she reread the settlements and recalled Mark's comments, she gave a disbelieving laugh. The estate was entailed, and so Mark inherited both the title and Fairhaven as well as a continued interest in the business, which in itself was no small thing. But Justin's fortune had been enormous, and Claudia had inherited it all, and after her, any heirs of her body. Claudia had shed tears at this evidence of her husband's loving hope that she might one day marry again. She had no intention of doing so. But Mark must have been furious, not relieved, to see such a proviso.

Two years after her husband's death, however, Claudia found herself coming back to life. She was beginning to find her time with her parents boring. Her mother was very much in charge of her own household and Claudia had little or nothing to do with herself. At first that had been a relief, but then it began to drive her to distraction. She could, of course, have gone back to Fairhaven. Mark had more than once invited her, but it was not a welcome prospect, nor did it seem quite within the bounds of propriety. She was his second cousin by marriage, but she was also his contemporary.

She finally decided to purchase a town house and move to London for the fall and spring Seasons. Her parents protested, but she was adamant, and so, at thirty-four, she was finally to have a "come-out." Not that she and Justin hadn't been to London often, and not, she told herself, that she was interested in a second marriage, but this would be the first time she would be taking part in the activities as an unattached, eligible woman. Not a young woman, it was true. But a very rich one.

Lady Fairhaven was an immediate success. She had always been very well liked for herself and respected for her obvious devotion to her older husband. But she had always stood in his shadow. She was now her own woman, self-assured and still very attractive.

The petite blonde beauty that had attracted the earl had changed little, except to mature and ripen. There were few lines in her face and she could have worn the dresses she had at seventeen, so little had her figure changed.

"Of course, why should she have wrinkles?" complained one society matron who was of an age with Claudia. "Justin Halesworth positively doted on her. She was cosseted all their married life."

"And never a child to thicken her waistline," observed another.

"But to give her credit, she is not fast, like Lady Montague, nor high in the instep, although she could be with all that money," said their companion.

The three ladies agreed that, as rich widows went, Lady Fairhaven was the most likable they had met.

The gentlemen were no less taken with her. A few, like Colonel Blunt and the Viscount Margate, were clearly after her money. And then there was young Littlefield, just down from Oxford, who was clearly in the throes of calf love. But at the beginning of the Season, her most frequent partner was her cousin-in-law, Mark Halesworth.

At first, Claudia was not at all surprised he sought her out. It was, after all, the polite and kindly thing to do. But after the first two weeks or so, Claudia began to notice that Mark was holding her just a little closer than was necessary for the waltz. And bending over her far more solicitously than she was comfortable with as he handed her a supper plate or a glass of punch. His warmth seemed real, but she still didn't trust him. Nor was she at all attracted to him. Thank God, he resembled his mother more than Justin's side of the family, but she had never liked his pale complexion or his thin-lipped, angular face. She wondered what was on his mind, and thought she knew. What could be better, from Mark's point of view, than that he unite both title and fortune by marrying his cousin's widow? Well, it was unfortunate for Mark that he was the last person in the world she would choose as a second husband. Not that she wanted one, but if she did, it would be someone who had a wide and generous mouth, like Anthony Varden.

She had met Tony Varden several weeks into the Season and felt an immediate sympathy for him. He too had lost someone he loved: first his father and then his older brother. She arranged an introduction to him with no great difficulty or comment, and accepted his polite offer to take her in to supper. While they sat together, she offered her condolences. Her words, while conventional, were so clearly heartfelt that he was quite touched. It was the first time that anyone had offered him sympathy for himself alone. All the others, including Joanna, had been suffering their own loss and wanting comfort as well as giving it. This woman seemed to see right through to his heart. To know that he had suffered, was suffering. He stammered out a thank-you, his usual insouciance deserting him.

The next time, he sought her out. And this time really looked at her. True, she was a few years older than he, but she most certainly didn't look it. In fact, she was one of the most attractive women in the room.

At first, he only set out to be charming to her to keep his mind off his worries. But as the Season wore on, he liked her more and more. She seemed to understand him. And she was refreshingly unsophisticated for a widow. He was sure that she had never been unfaithful to Lord Fairhaven.

There were a few fellows hanging around her, but he easily dismissed them as rivals. As he dismissed Mark Halesworth. Halesworth was being very solicitous, to be sure, but he was a cold fish. Tony had known him at school, where he'd been a few years Mark's junior. Mark had had a reputation for real cruelty to younger boys. Tony had been lucky enough to keep out of his way, but he had heard enough stories to make him form an instant dislike.

He couldn't imagine Lady Fairhaven could really like the fellow, so he managed to rescue her from his company as often as he could within the bounds of polite behavior. And by the end of the first half of the Season, gossips were speculating about Lord Ashford and Lady Fairhaven.

One afternoon in early May, Mark was announced to his cousin. A slight frown creased her brow when her butler handed her Mark's card, but she put on a polite smile and had him shown in.

"Good afternoon, Claudia. You are looking quite lovely today."

"Thank you, Mark." Years ago she had stopped him from calling her "Cousin Claudia," which had sounded ridiculous. It still would, of course, but she would have welcomed the distance it would have suggested. The more attention Mark paid her, the more uncomfortable she felt with him.

"I am not come on a social visit, Claudia."

"Oh?"

"No. I am here as a member of your family to express the concern I have about your welfare."

Claudia lifted her teacup and took a measured swallow, while gesturing to her butler to serve her cousin.

"And what concern is that, Mark?" she asked evenly. Inside she was seething. Express his concern, indeed! How dare he presume to tell her what to do? For she knew that was what he was about. Mark was too cold to feel anything, much less concern for her welfare.

"I have noticed, as indeed have others, that you are spending more time with Tony Varden than with any other gentlemen. I am worried about you. My cousin kept you very protected, you know, and you are relatively inexperienced in the ways of the world. Ashford is good-looking and charming, it is true, so I am aware of his appeal. Especially for a woman whose first husband was so much older than she. But his interest in you can be nothing but financial. I am sorry to be so blunt, Claudia. But you are a very wealthy woman, and as such, prey to all kinds of fortune hunters."

"You mean like Blunt and Margate?"

"Why, yes, they are certainly two of the worst."

"And you think that I am too old and wrinkled to appeal to Lord Ashford for any other reason than my money?"

Mark set his cup down and took one of Claudia's hands in his. "Of course not. You are one of the most attractive women in London."

Claudia slipped her hand out of his. "But I am older than he."

"You are. And more to the point, he has recently inherited an impoverished title and estate."

"I know that, Mark."

"But do you also know that his strategy for bringing the estate back is to frequent the gaming hells? He is an inveterate gambler, Claudia, and I have it on good authority that he is badly dipped."

Claudia kept her face expressionless. She had known, of course, about Tony's inheritance. And he had confessed to her himself his unsuitability for the responsibilities he carried. He had compared himself to his brother more than once, and she had responded with the instant sympathy he drew from her and reassured him.

She had heard some whispering about his gambling, but had dismissed it as malicious gossip. She had never seen him sit down at a card table on any occasion they were together. It was true that he often looked tired, but she had put that down to his worries about his family. It was also true that he did not usually attend more than one or two social functions in an evening, nor stay until the early morning hours. She had always assumed that he was just being conscientious about his attempts to set his affairs in order.

"And what 'good authority' is that, Mark? I have heard some of the gossip myself, but have seen nothing in Lord Ashford to indicate such an obsession."

"I heard it from one of the blacklegs himself, one Boniface, who works at Seventy-Five St. James Street. Tony is there almost every night, winning and losing at Rouge et Noir . . . mostly losing. I do not want you to be hurt, Claudia. I . . . care about you very much, you know."

"And I you," Claudia responded very matter-of-factly. "I am glad to have a relative of Justin's to advise me."

"I would like to be able to do more than just advise you, Claudia." Mark's expression changed. Claudia supposed that the thin-lipped smile and the expectant lift of his eyebrows was to suggest warmer feeling for her. But there was no warmth in his eyes. She stood up and walked to the window, avoiding the hand stretched out to . . . well, she didn't know what his hand was going to do. Perhaps only pat her hand again. Her back was to him for a moment, and so she couldn't see his expression change. His lips were pressed together and every bit of the coldness she suspected was present in his eyes. But his face softened as she turned.

"Mark, I very much appreciate your solicitousness. I will certainly think hard about what you have told me. I would even make some discreet inquiries of my own, were I contemplating a second marriage. But I am not. Perhaps in a few years I will feel differently, but right now, Justin's memory is too tender for me to consider anyone in his place."

"Of course, Claudia. Forgive me if I have unintentionally caused you any embarrassment."

"Not at all, Mark." Claudia reached out and took his offered hand and squeezed it gratefully. "I know exactly where your concern was coming from."

A minute after he was gone, Claudia looked up at the portrait of her late husband that hung over the fireplace.

"I never had the courage to say this before, Justin, but your cousin is a self-serving, cold-hearted . . . *toad*. And if you *did* set up your will to encourage an understanding between us, then that is the only stupid thing I have ever known you to do. Concerned for me, indeed! The only thing Mark Halesworth is concerned about is money. Don't look at me like that, Justin. I know that as a wealthy widow I am at risk. But there is something about Lord Ashford that draws me to him. And I have been very lonely without you, my dear."

4

Mark left the house feeling somewhat reassured. He knew that Claudia had loved his cousin, and although it had been two years since Justin's death, it was possible that she felt no desire to remarry. That did not mean she never would. But if she did, he meant to see that she married him.

When he was very young, Mark was not fully aware of how close he was to the earldom. His mother did not speak of it much, although she always carefully checked Justin's letters for any references to eligible European women, and when she found none, would fold them up with a sigh of relief. But as Mark got older and Justin remained single, his mother encouraged him to think of himself as heir to everything: title, estate, and business. And Mark did. In school, he acted as though he were already the earl, and only socialized with older sons. He took his position so for granted that when news of the marriage reached him at school he lost not a moment's sleep over it. But when he returned home that summer, his mother's reaction began to wake him up to the reality: Lord Fairhaven had married a much younger woman and would likely produce an heir.

When he made his courtesy visit, he began to take his mother's complaining seriously. He would watch his doting cousin with his new bride, and the resentment planted by his mother grew.

Summer after summer went by, with Mark watching for signs that Lady Fairhaven might be increasing. After seven years and no heir, Mark began to relax. And when, a few years after that, Justin tacitly acknowledged him, introducing him to estate matters, Mark again began to take for granted that he would get what was due him when the earl died. And he deserved it, damn it, after all these years of waiting and insecurity.

His cold hostility toward Claudia, which he had kept very well hidden, began to diminish. After all, she kept his cousin happy. She would probably inherit a tidy amount, go off to London, and marry again.

No one was more surprised than Mark when the will was read, and no one hid it better. He offered both his sympathy and congratulations and acted as though he had only expected the title and estate. After all, he had made quite a bit of money in his position as manager already, since like the late earl, he was a shrewd investor.

His mother was beyond consolation, however. "I can't believe Justin would do this to you," she cried, when they reached the privacy of her home. "To raise our expectations all these years and then to give it all away to that devious little conniver."

"Claudia is hardly that, Mother," responded her son. "Even you must admit that she was devoted to Cousin Justin. Her grief is quite genuine."

Mrs. Halesworth, whose temperament was volatile, burst into tears and cried out that she was a terrible cousin-in-law indeed to be thinking of money at a sad time like this.

Mark, whose reserve had developed as a reaction to his mother's tendency to overdramatize every little shift in her emotions, patted her shoulder automatically and waited for her to dry her eyes.

"Although, Mark, I wonder . . . she said, lifting her head, her face transformed once again. "Fairhaven cared about you very much. Look at how he paid for your education and promoted you so quickly. Perhaps the will was his way of suggesting—which he could never have done in any other way, of course—that the title and fortune come together through you and Claudia?"

Mark might work to keep himself aloof from his mother,

but that didn't mean she hadn't a strong influence on him. The opposite, in fact. He had allowed himself to believe he would inherit everything. And now? Well, there was a certain sense in what she said. Who better to marry Claudia than the new earl?

As his hostility to Claudia had decreased over the years, he couldn't help noticing that she was a very attractive woman. He didn't love her. He couldn't imagine his emotions binding him to any woman in that way. But he could imagine bedding her for a while, until he had his heir.

There was no rush. She wouldn't return to society for at least a year.

He had been a little surprised by her two-year stay with her parents, but was in no way disappointed, for it meant her grief was even deeper than he could have guessed, and therefore she wasn't likely to rush into a second marriage.

And so, when she purchased the town house and came up to London for her first Season as an unattached woman, he only saw it as his opportunity to win her hand. He had to admit she didn't seem particularly drawn to him. But neither was she drawn to anyone else. Until Tony Varden.

Varden was the fly in the ointment. He was handsome enough, Mark had to admit, if you liked the combination of merry brown eyes, which could turn serious in an instant, above a sensuous full mouth. And women did seem to like it. And the unusual combination of blond hair with dark eyes.

Claudia certainly looked happy enough in Varden's arms, thought Mark, after he left the town house. She looked very comfortable as his dance partner and very absorbed in conversation at suppers and musicales. Varden had done nothing to put the relationship on a more physical basis, to Mark's knowledge. That didn't mean, of course, that nothing was happening. Claudia was an independent widow, not a hedged-in virgin up for her first Season. For all Mark knew, Varden could be visiting every night. Except that he couldn't, thought Mark, because he was spending all his time at 75 St. James. That little bit of information was true, and despite Claudia's disclaimer, he was sure he had affected her opinion of Varden.

But he needed to keep a close eye on his seemingly virtuous cousin. If he only had someone inside her household who could inform him about her relationship with Varden . . . He could buy off one of the under-footmen, and then introduce his own replacement to her. He had just the man, he realized. One Jim Rooke, who worked in the warehouse as an assistant clerk. His parents had been in service and saw Jim's employment as a step up for the family. He was an ambitious young man, from what Mark knew of him, and if he was offered a bonus and a promotion, was sure to jump at the chance to please his employer. As a footman, Jim could keep his eyes and ears open for gossip about Lady Fairhaven and Lord Ashford. A spy in Claudia's household was just what he needed.

5

By mid-Season, it was clear to anyone who had eyes that Lord Ashford was devoting almost as much time to his pursuit of Lady Fairhaven as to Rouge et Noir. Although perhaps "pursuit" was not the right word, since the lady was not running anywhere. And if it came to a match, well, it would make perfect sense for all concerned, said the gossips. Lady Fairhaven was rich enough to rescue Lord Ashford and his family and hardly note the expenditure. And he was, after all, a very handsome young man. Younger man. After her first marriage, she was probably looking to please herself.

Tony was aware of the gossip. He knew what it looked like: Desperate young man charms wealthy widow and marries her to obtain her fortune. And, unfortunately, there was some truth in what it looked like. After their first conversation, Tony had felt a growing bond between them, and with her money in mind, *had* used his considerable charm to strengthen their friendship. But it was a real friendship. At least on his part. He *liked* Claudia and he admired her. She could have acted like many a young woman married to an older man and found a young lover. Instead, she had opened her heart to the possibilities in her marriage and made it a happy one.

She was also a very pretty woman and hardly looked five years his senior.

He wasn't quite sure what her feelings toward him were. Their liking was mutual. But he suspected from a few unguarded glances that she might be more romantically inclined than he. He had much to offer her in exchange for her fortune: affection, companionship, youth . . . but not passion. And he suspected that rich as her first marriage may have been, it had probably lacked that. But the only passion Tony was capable of right now, he admitted to himself, was for the cards. Well, of course, not the cards themselves, but for what they could do for himself and his family: restore Ashford and give Ned's death meaning. But it was time to discover if his affection for Lady Fairhaven might include the physical.

That night at the Faradays' ball, Tony secured two waltzes and Claudia's hand for supper. After their first dance, he let his hand stay around her waist for a minute or so after he escorted her off the dance floor, and Claudia made no move to step away. He delivered her to her next partner and sought out Joanna, who was standing on the sidelines with her parents.

"Not dancing tonight, Joanna?" he teased.

"My card is empty for this dance, Tony," she replied blandly. She would not look either arch or pleading. Not that Tony would notice anyway. He seemed to have eyes only for Lady Fairhaven.

"Lord, but Fairhaven is stiff," muttered Tony, for Claudia was dancing with Mark.

"He is not at all a good partner for Lady Fairhaven," agreed Joanna, watching Claudia's graceful movements. She was petite and pretty, with a delectable figure: everything the tall and average-looking Joanna was not. No wonder Tony was interested.

"No, he is not a partner I would recommend, on or off the dance floor," continued Tony.

"I must confess, I had not thought of that," said Joanna. "Do you think that there is any possibility of a match? It would be to both their advantages, after all. He would get her fortune and her son, if she had one, would inherit the earldom. Not that he really needs her money," Joanna added. "Managing the late earl's business enabled him to become very comfortable."

Tony frowned. It was true. Halesworth was rich enough on his own, although it was nothing compared to what Claudia had inherited. But if Fairhaven was as greedy as he was cold, then he might well be thinking of pursuing Claudia. In that case, his own pursuit of the lady could almost be viewed as an act of chivalry. Surely she deserved a better second husband than Mark Halesworth.

"I doubt that Mark would appeal to her," said Tony, turning and smiling at Joanna. "Perhaps she will be looking for something more in her second husband than a good head for business."

Joanna's heart sank. She knew Tony well, and that gleam in his eye meant that he had one more reason to pursue Lady Fairhaven. He would not have hinted at all, were he not interested.

"There is some gossip that you are interested in the lady, Tony. Everyone has noticed your attentions to her. Has someone conquered your heart at last?" she asked, keeping her voice light. She knew it would hurt, but she had to know.

"I am sure that the gossips are not claiming that my heart is in her hands."

"No," Joanna admitted. "They are saying that you have lost so much at the tables that you must marry Lady Fairhaven or lose Ashford. Is that true, Tony?" she asked quietly, dreading the answer. Somehow, no matter how much it would hurt, she would rather Tony have lost his heart than his integrity. She thought she could bear his falling in love with another woman, for she had almost given up hope that he would ever feel that way about her. But she did not think she could stand losing all her respect for him. She knew his weaknesses better than anyone, but she had not thought they included complete lack of control over his impulses, or cynicism so deep that he would marry a woman for her money. Then again, who could tell what his father's and brother's deaths had done to him? Weakness in one setting was often a strength in another, and she was sure that he was at his best in the army. Not as the Earl of Ashford.

"Of course not. I am surprised you would listen to such gossip, Joanna." Tony's face was flushed as he made his denial. "I may have lost a little here and there, but my luck is beginning to turn. And I would never marry where there is no affection. I like Lady Fairhaven very much, as a matter-of-fact, and if I did ask her to be my wife, it would be for that reason, and no other."

Joanna believed he was telling the truth. Almost. She was sure he did have some affection for Lady Fairhaven. She was also sure that the gossips were not wrong. That flush had betrayed him. He was deeply in debt and unable to come about in any other way than marrying a woman with a great deal of money. For one moment, Joanna imagined grabbing his arm and saying: "Tony, if you are thinking of marrying to secure Ashford, then why not me?" But although her portion was decent and she could expect a small inheritance from her grandmother when she married, it was nothing to the size of Lady Fairhaven's fortune. And nowhere near enough to save Ashford.

Tony gave a mock groan, which shook Joanna out of her depressing thoughts. "Look at me, standing here jabbering to you about my problems when instead I should have asked you to dance. No wonder you look bored. Will you give me another chance later, Jo?"

"Unfortunately, this was my only free dance, Lord Varden. You have missed your chance, I am afraid," replied Joanna with patrician hauteur, happy to be back in the familiar teasing mode in which she and her old friend generally communicated.

"A good setdown. Well, put me down for a waltz at Lady Pembroke's tomorrow."

"I will, my lord."

"Is it young Dracut who has your hand for the next country dance?"

"Yes."

"Well, here he comes. I think I will leave you to him, my dear. He is so full of energy that he makes me feel positively ancient!"

Joanna watched Dracut approach and willed herself not to follow Tony across the room, where he was, of course, approaching Lady Fairhaven. She turned on her brightest smile and prepared herself for her bumptious partner.

Tony had put himself down for a country dance with Claudia on purpose. It was very warm inside the ballroom and he was hoping the exertion would make her welcome a suggestion to seek an open window on one of the balconies.

And indeed, after the dance ended, Claudia was very pink and fanned herself vigorously.

"It is uncommonly hot tonight," said Tony solicitously. "Perhaps we could seek some fresh air for a moment or two?"

Claudia glanced up quickly and then immediately lowered her eyes and nodded her assent. It *was* warm, but usually couples sought the balconies to generate heat, rather than to get away from it. Up until now, Tony had been very careful with his physical attentions: his arm lingering around her waist, or a slight squeeze of the hand. Considering she was a widow and not some green girl, he had been very thoughtful. But she suspected that was about to change.

When they reached the balcony, Tony left the door into the ballroom open, and leaning against the railing, made witty observations for a few minutes about the couples they could see whirling around on the dance floor. Claudia was disappointed. Perhaps he had been interested only in fresh air!

But then he stepped away from the railing and closed the door more than halfway behind her.

"I have been hoping for a while that you would give me permission to call you Claudia, my dear," he said, moving closer.

"I am not sure that would be appropriate, my lord. After all, we do not know each other that well."

"Ah, but I do not intend to leave this balcony before becoming better acquainted." Tony reached out, and grasping her hands, pulled Claudia even closer. Her head only reached his chest, and despite the difference in their ages, this made him feel protective. He put his finger under her chin and lifted her face to his. Claudia turned away quickly in embarrassment, and then gave a surprised gasp of pain.

"What is it?" asked Tony with concern. Surely he couldn't have frightened her?

"My earring. It is caught." Tony leaned down and smiled to see her dangling ear-bob tangled in a tendril of hair.

"Hold still," he whispered. He had to lean very close to see what he was doing, and the sensation of his warm breath on her neck was delightful. She could feel him tug on her ear as he gently pulled the earring free. But when she could tell it was again hanging as it should, he did not move away, but kept his hand in her hair.

"Now I am caught," he said, as he ran his fingers through her curls. She shivered.

"Surely you could not be cold, my lady?"

"No, Lord . . . Tony, I am not cold."

"Do you shiver in anticipation of this?" he asked, and turning her head towards him, he kissed her gently on the lips. Her mouth opened immediately under his, and their kiss became more passionate. After a moment or two, Tony pulled back. "Do you wish to go back inside, Claudia?"

"Not yet, Tony."

This time she reached her arms up and pulled him down to her. Their kiss was long and deep, and when Claudia felt him run his thumb gently under her breast she thought her insides were dissolving.

When they finally broke apart, she laughed shakily and reached up to straighten his cravat.

"Yes, well, you look a bit disheveled too, my lady."

Claudia reached up again, this time to smooth her hair.

"Your gown too," said Tony, with a wicked gleam in his

eye. "Here, let me," and he pulled the bodice of her gown back in place.

"Claudia, I want you to know that I do not make a habit of attacking young women on balconies."

"What about older women, my lord?" she teased.

Tony blushed. "Truly, I never think of you as older, Claudia, although I know you are by a year or two."

"Five."

"Why, that is nothing, my dear. And you don't look a day over . . . ."

"Thirty-four. I am thirty-four, Tony, and you are twenty-nine."

"Age does not matter, Claudia. Not when there is affection and attraction. Do you really care what other people think?"

"Not about our ages, Tony, but there is other gossip," said Claudia hesitantly.

"You mean that I am a desperate young man with a ruined estate, pursuing you for your wealth," Tony replied, his expression set and serious.

"Yes."

"Is that what you think me, Claudia?"

"I *am* a very wealthy widow, Tony."

"I am not going to pretend that your money does not matter to me, Claudia. You know my family's situation. But there are at least two other available widows this Season, my dear. If I were only interested in money, I would be spreading my charms around to see whom I could trap first. The truth is, I have felt a special sympathy between us, my lady."

Tony said "My lady" not as though it was merely a courtesy. He said it caressingly as though it were true: that she was his lady.

"As have I, Tony. We both know what it is to lose someone we love. And although you are not that much younger than I am, you remind me a little of my younger self, too early saddled with responsibility."

"Twenty-nine is hardly comparable to seventeen, Claudia. I am not a boy, but a seasoned soldier," said Tony, sounding mildly insulted.

"I do not mean to offend you, Tony. I am not sure I can explain it myself." She could, but she feared he would not want to hear that she sensed that a part of him was still seventeen or so, carefree and dreaming about freedom and the glory to be gained on the battlefield. As a younger son, he had always been somewhat in limbo, with nothing to be committed to or responsible for except himself.

"I care very much about you, Claudia. I want to—"

"And I care for you, Tony," Claudia interrupted. "And I also find you impossibly attractive. But may we leave it there just for now?"

"As long as you know that my intentions are honorable."

"I know they are, my lord," Claudia replied softly. She had stopped what was surely a proposal because she was afraid she would have said yes before he even finished. She wanted him that much. But although she was quite desperately in love with him, she wasn't ready to give her life over into his hands. Not until she found out how hopelessly he was entangled in his gaming.

6

Mark Halesworth had seen them go out onto the balcony and had completely ignored his dance partner as he watched over her shoulder. When Tony pulled the doors partly closed, his hand tightened convulsively around his partner's and she winced with pain.

"I apologize, Miss Hall, I was distracted."

And when Claudia and Tony emerged, looking no cooler than when they had sought the fresh air, Mark knew that the time had come to take some action.

The next evening, Mark left his office when it closed, a very unusual thing for him to do. Although he had hired someone to take his place as manager when he'd inherited the title, he found it hard to give up control. He visited two or three times a week, often not leaving until eight or nine. In fact, he had even had a small dressing room and wardrobe set up in his office so that he could dress and go directly to a ball or the theatre without having to return home.

What was even more unusual was that he headed for the Crown, a small pub a few blocks away. When he got there, he took a seat in the darkest corner and surveyed the bar. When the barmaid approached him, he ordered an ale and also bought a drink for one of the young men at the bar.

When the young man turned to thank him, Mark waved him over to the table.

"Why, your lordship, it is you! Thank you for the drink, my lord."

"Come, sit down, Jim."

Jim looked flustered. "Oh, no, I couldn't do that, my lord."

"I insist," said Mark in a voice that no one who was in his employ ignored.

"Thank you, sir," said Jim, and sat.

"How long have you been with the business, Jim?"

Jim's heart sank. As a relatively new clerk and lowest on the totem pole, he felt quite vulnerable. He had made his share of mistakes. Perhaps Lord Fairhaven had only bought him a drink to make a dismissal less painful.

"Only seven months, my lord."

"And you are happy with your position?"

"Oh, yes, my lord."

"Although an assistant clerk is unlikely to get rich."

"No, my lord. I mean yes, my lord, I *do* like it. And I hadn't intended to stay an assistant forever," Jim added boldly.

"Your parents were in service, I understand?"

Jim was surprised. He hadn't thought Lord Fairhaven the type to care where his lesser employees came from.

"Why, yes, my lord. They worked for Lord and Lady Summers."

"A very refined household. And they sent you to school?"

"They didn't want me to follow them into service, my lord. They wanted me to get on further than they had."

"And here you are, at Halesworth Limited."

"Yes, my lord. And hoping to be there for a long time." Why not say it, thought Jim. If he was going to be dismissed anyway, it couldn't hurt. Maybe it would help.

"I certainly hope so. In fact, I have a proposition to make to you that would ensure you a promotion."

Jim took a great swallow of ale. He wasn't going to be dismissed? He was going to be promoted? But so soon?

"I would be happy to do anything I could for you, my lord."

"Good lad," said Mark, smiling over at him.

The ale and the relief combined to make Jim very relaxed. Until now, Lord Fairhaven had seemed a hard man of business. Maybe they had all misjudged him, however. Maybe his harsh exterior was only—

"I want you to leave the warehouse."

Jim's heart sank again. Lord Fairhaven was playing a cruel joke. He had only raised Jim's hopes to crush them entirely.

"Temporarily, of course, Jim. And when you return, you will be a senior clerk."

"I don't understand, my lord."

"I still want you in my employ, Jim, but it will be rather indirectly. I want you to apply for the position as underfootman in Lady Fairhaven's household."

"Your rich widowed cousin?" Jim realized what he'd said and blurted out an apology.

"That is quite all right, Jim. She *is* a rich widow. And that is exactly why I need someone there to keep an eye on her. My cousin was very fond of her. Well, so am I, for that matter. She is my only family, aside from my mother. And she has been spending a great deal of time with a very inappropriate—nay, dangerous—young man. I need someone in her household whom I can trust. Someone who can tell me exactly what her relationship to the Earl of Ashford is."

"The Earl of Ashford? Aren't his pockets completely to let?"

"You have heard of him, then?"

"Well, my lord, my parents are retired, but they still hear all the town gossip from their old friends. I know that the earl recently inherited the title."

"And a bankrupt estate. I am afraid he is a fortune hunter, only after Lady Fairhaven's money. And he is desperate, because he has foolishly been trying to recoup his fortune in the gaming hells. I believe he owes a great deal of money. You can see why I am concerned about my cousin?"

"Oh, yes, my lord," Jim answered, feeling sympathy already for Lady Fairhaven.

"Now, if you were in the household, you would be able to tell me whether Ashford is getting anywhere in his suit. Even whether he spends the night. You understand?"

"Yes, my lord. You need a sort of domestic spy."

"Exactly."

Jim frowned. "I don't like invading a lady's privacy," he said hesitantly.

"Neither do I, Jim. But it is for her own good, isn't it? I only want to keep her from making a disastrous match, in which she might have her fortune drained away and her heart broken."

"I do admire your motive," Jim admitted.

"And you are the perfect man for the job. A young man whose parents were in service, so he needs very little training. And a talented clerk, who will be rewarded with a raise and a promotion. How can you refuse?"

Indeed, Jim could not. So it was agreed that he would leave the warehouse in a few days and apply at Lady Fairhaven's household. Jim went home dazed by his good fortune, thinking what a happy coincidence it was that there was an opening for a footman in Lady Fairhaven's household precisely at the time his employer needed him there. And Mark went on to his next errand, which was to give Lady Fairhaven's under-footman a substantial amount of compensation for leaving his position the next morning.

7

Tony lifted his shirts and gazed at the leather bag of guineas which he had hidden in the drawer. One hundred guineas, which he had promised himself were untouchable. Proof that he was in control, not the cards. Then he looked at his shirts and smiled humorlessly. He could sell one, like young Lindsay, he supposed. After all, it was not his last and would not be off his back.

There was no possibility of convincing the bank to advance him any money. He had already spent his allowance from the rent of the town house, which was ridiculously meager for an earl. But Ned, God damn him or God bless him, Tony wasn't sure what he felt this evening, had set things up so that the little that was left of the Ashford fortune went right back into the estate. Of course, as the new earl, Tony could have overridden his brother's actions, but not without alerting Farley and his mother to their situation. He pulled out the bag and counted out twenty-five guineas. The cards had been so bad for these past few nights that things had to get better. He would only take twenty-five. Seventy-five would stay untouchable. And he would win tonight, he was sure. And go on winning. After all, if fortunes were lost at the tables, they could also be won. And he didn't see why he shouldn't be the winner.

He *was* lucky that night. He came home with a hundred and thirty pounds. Twenty-five went back in the bag and the rest would be his seed money for the next night. But the next night he lost all, and had to sign vowels for fifty-three pounds. Well, fifty-three guineas still left forty-seven. Except that he needed at least twenty-five to start winning again . . .

By the end of the week he had seven guineas left in the leather bag, which lay there as shrunken as an old cow's udder. He was beginning to feel desperate. He had already touched his friends for twenty pounds here and there and owed them as well as tradesmen all over town.

He could ask Claudia for a loan, but he hated to do it. Their friendship was in the process of evolving into something more intimate. He had kissed her again, and her response was so gratifying that he was beginning to think he could be very happy as her husband. And from what he could see, she was already in love with him.

If he hadn't liked her so much, hadn't been genuinely drawn to her ripe beauty, he would have felt like only another fortune hunter. But he *did* like her and was sure he could make her a good husband. Perhaps even give her a child, which Fairhaven had never been able to do. No, marrying Lady Fairhaven for the money to save Ashford did not make him feel guilty at all. But to ask her to clear up his gambling debts did. She didn't really know the state of his pockets and he didn't want her to.

But if he proposed within the next few weeks and she accepted, then he wouldn't need to return to 75 St. James again. After all, he had started that before he had met her, when he thought the only way to clear the estate was through the cards. He would assure her of that, obtain a small, one-time-only loan, and then make her his betrothed.

It was only one, a bit early for a morning call, but Tony decided to take care of things right away, and so he dressed carefully, brushed his wayward curls into some kind of order, and set out for Lady Fairhaven's.

He was admitted by the new under-footman, a slim young man who hadn't quite mastered the haughty demeanor of a town servant yet.

"Would you please give my card to Lady Fairhaven and ask if she will see me, James."

"Yes, my lord." Another visit to report, thought Jim, who had been there for over a week. A little early, but Jim had already reported that Lord Ashford was visiting almost daily. And that a few evenings he had escorted Lady Fairhaven home and stayed for longer than a nightcap called for, leaving Lady Fairhaven looking as though something other than brandy had made her cheeks flushed and her eyes slightly dazed.

He announced Lord Ashford and watched his mistress's face light up. "Thank you, James," she said warmly. She was a nice woman, Lady Fairhaven, thought Jim, as he opened the door for her. One who seemed to care for her servants, even the newest ones. For the first few days, Jim had felt guilty indeed about his spying. Then, as he began to get to know her better and feel a real affection for her, he began to see himself less a spy and more her protector. After all, the whole reason for this was to make sure she didn't succumb to the wiles of a handsome young fortune hunter like Lord Ashford. Who was even more badly dipped this week than usual, if downstairs gossip was to be believed.

He led the way to the drawing room and opened the door for Lady Fairhaven. He saw Lord Ashford get up and approach her, taking her hands in his, and then had to close the door behind them and resume his post in the front hall.

"Tony, what a pleasant surprise. I didn't think I was going to see you until tonight."

Tony dropped a kiss on the top of Claudia's head and then led her over to the sofa, but stayed standing even after she sat down.

He cleared his throat nervously and then said: "I am not going to beat around the bush, Claudia. I have something important to ask you."

Claudia could feel her heart beating faster. Was he going to propose today? She knew it was where they had been heading these past few weeks. And she thought she knew what her answer would be. Despite the rumors and despite the difference in their ages, she knew that Tony cared about her, that she was in love with him, and that they were attracted to each other. A better basis for marriage than most, surely.

"You know my situation, Claudia. I've told you what a responsibility fell on my shoulders when Ned died."

She nodded.

"When I first came to London, I thought . . . now I see it was foolish, of course, but I was so overwhelmed . . . I *have* been gambling as much as they say. I never was much of a player before, so I am not sure why it has such a hold on me. I suppose it is Ashford. Anyway, I am not trying to make excuses. And I am determined to stop."

Claudia smiled up at him. "I am very glad, Tony. I have heard rumors, but didn't want to believe them."

"Yes, well . . ." Tony turned away. Clearly he was making this difficult confession to clear the way for his proposal, she thought. "But before I stop," he continued, "I must pay off my debts. I hate to ask you this, Claudia, but I need to borrow six hundred pounds . . . er, guineas."

Claudia's heart sank. She had so wanted him to be leading up to a declaration. She had so wanted to throw her arms around his neck and be lost in his embrace. And to relax again, knowing that she once again had a protector.

But then, Tony was not Justin, she reminded herself. And she was no seventeen-year-old girl. And standing in front of her was that boy whom she sensed in Tony, who was at last trying to grow up. And wouldn't she prefer the eventual proposal (for she knew it would come) from a man?

"Exactly how much do you need, Tony?" she asked quietly.

"Six hundred guineas would clear everything."

"All right. I will send to the bank this afternoon and have it delivered directly."

"Claudia, you don't know how ashamed I am to be taking this from you."

"Nonsense. We are good friends, aren't we? We care about one another. Well, good friends help one another out." Claudia wanted no shame-ridden gratitude to taint their relationship. "Now let us put this behind us. Do you go to Lord Roth's tonight?"

"For a short while. Then I will have to go to St. James Street to clear myself."

"Of course," Claudia murmured.

"But we will have a waltz and supper together at Devonshire House tomorrow."

"I will look forward to that, then."

"I must go, Claudia. But I thank you, my lady, with all my heart, for your generous friendship." The look in Tony's eyes more than compensated for the few moments of disappointment on the sofa.

8

Jim stood on the corner, waiting for the hansom cab to pick him up. He was a few blocks from the house, but shuffled his feet nervously, for another servant might come by at any time. He was relieved to see the cab approaching and have the door opened for him from the inside.

"Good afternoon, your lordship," he said as he settled into the cab.

"Good afternoon, Jim. Do you have anything new to report to me?"

Jim felt very important as he nodded solemnly and said, "Indeed I do, my lord."

Fairhaven's eyes narrowed, and when Jim looked into his face a sort of shiver went through him at the predatory look on his employer's face. He hesitated for a moment, but then remembered he was not feeding mice to an impatient cat, but giving a member of Lady Fairhaven's family information that might save her from an irredeemable mistake.

"Well?" Fairhaven demanded sharply.

"Lord Ashford visited Lady Fairhaven early yesterday afternoon. Of course I couldn't overhear their conversation, but William, the upper-footman, told me that he had been sent to cash a bank draft for over six hundred guineas and then directed to deliver the money to Lord Ashford. I am sure that Ashford came for the express purpose of begging money."

"So he is finally showing his true colors," said Fairhaven, with great satisfaction. "I knew that my cousin was in danger, Jim. I admit that I hated to hire a spy, but I needed to know that my suspicions had some basis. Now I know they do."

"I have become very devoted to her ladyship," Jim volunteered hesitantly. "Any reservations about my job are quite gone now."

Fairhaven drew a guinea out of his pocket. "Here is a bonus for your work, Jim. I will find some way to put this information to good use." He ordered the cab to let him down at the next corner and returned home in a far happier mood than he had been for days.

That night, he too was to be at Devonshire House, and left his office early in order to stop at his club, something he rarely did. It was his lucky day, he decided, for not only did he have Jim's piece of information, but when he entered, all the talk was of how Tony Varden had dropped almost six hundred guineas at Rouge et Noir last night.

"And you know Tony," said one of Ashford's acquaintances proudly. "He never turned a hair. Cool as you please, he kept betting the black. Won a little at first, but even when he started losing, his expression never changed. Down five hundred seventy guineas and he spent the rest treating the house to champagne, as if he were a winner, not a loser. God knows where he got the money to play with to begin with."

"Rumor has it, from a certain not-so-young widow," said another, not realizing who had just walked in behind him.

"Are you referring to Lady Fairhaven?" asked Mark coldly.

"Er . . . not especifically, why no, of course not."

"Good, for I would hate to have my cousin's name bandied about."

"Good God, Henry," said his friend as Mark moved on to the other room, "Watch what you say."

"Well, it is well known that Ashford is after her. And that she isn't running away. I'll bet it will be a match within a month."

"You are behind the times, Henry. I entered that bet in the books over two weeks ago. But I will bet that Ashford's gambling makes her think twice about marrying him. If she ain't careful, he'll go through her fortune."

When he got to Devonshire House, Mark found his cousin immediately and made sure to obtain a waltz with her later on in the evening. He danced with a few young ladies and made polite conversation, but most of his attention was taken up watching for Ashford's arrival.

When Mark went to claim Claudia for his waltz, Tony had still not arrived. No doubt he did not have the courage to face her, thought Mark, as he led Claudia onto the dance floor.

After the dance ended, he asked Claudia if she would like to go for a short walk in the garden. "You look a bit drawn, my dear," he added solicitously.

Claudia took one last look around the room and then thanked Mark and took his arm.

He was very careful not to move out of sight of the couples that were walking outside. He did not intend to betray his own interest yet. But he did make sure they were out of hearing when he sat Claudia down on a bench facing one corner of the knot garden.

"Claudia, I am hesitant to bring this up again, but I am worried about you and Ashford."

"Mark, we have already gone over this."

"I know, but last time we spoke, I had only heard second- and third-hand rumors about his gambling. I have seen your growing interest in him and it has worried me, but since I wish only for your happiness, I did not intend to say anything. Now I must. The news was all over my club that Ashford dropped almost six hundred guineas at the tables last night. Or five hundred and eighty, to be precise. The rest he spent in drinks for all and sundry," added Mark dryly.

He heard Claudia's sharp intake of breath and smiled to himself.

"There are wagers in the books on whether Ashford will succeed in winning a certain Lady F. I hate to have you treated in such a vulgar fashion, Claudia, but if you continue seeing Ashford, that is what you can expect." Mark hesitated. "I also couldn't help but wonder where Ashford got the money. He has never gone to the tables with that much before. You didn't fund him, did you, my dear?"

Claudia thought that she had never hated Mark Halesworth so much as at that moment. She was sure he didn't care at all for her reputation, but was more concerned with her feelings for Tony Varden. Underneath all his supposed concern she was sure he was gloating. She could feel it. *Now you see I was right, he was only after your money.* Except he didn't have the courage to say it straight out.

Underneath her fierce anger at Mark she was very hurt. How could Tony have promised and then gone right off to the tables? Were Mark and all the gossips right? Was there nothing to Tony but the fortune hunter and compulsive gamester? Had she completely deceived herself and seen affection where there was none, merely because she had fallen in love like a green girl? Well, whatever the truth was, she wasn't about to let Mark see it.

"I did give him the money. Not that it is anyone's business," Claudia answered coldly. "It is, after all, my money, and I can do with it as I wish."

"But surely you meant him to pay off his creditors, not throw it away on the table."

"I don't put conditions on my gifts, Mark. I had no idea what Tony wanted the money for," she lied.

"But now that you know? Surely you won't—"

"Won't what? Marry him? I will if he asks me. And if he doesn't, perhaps I will ask him," she added boldly. "You see, Tony and I are very good friends."

"Friendship is no basis for marriage, Claudia."

"We are more than just good friends, Mark. And I am a grown woman now. I can marry whomever I wish. And I wish to marry Tony Varden."

"I thought you and Cousin Justin were very happy together."

"Of course we were. But we might easily not have been, a seventeen-year-old girl and a forty-seven-year-old man. This time, I will do the choosing."

"You mean buying."

Claudia wanted to slap Mark across his self-satisfied face, but she resisted. As she stood up, she said: "I am going to marry Tony, Mark. And believe me, I will be very happy with a young husband. If you do not approve, that is your business, but I do not need your advice, however well meaning," she added, with some sarcasm. "Of course, if you cannot bring yourself to accept my decision, you need not visit. Now, please, I would like to go in."

Claudia smiled and chatted and danced for the rest of the evening, making sure that none would think her concerned by Tony's absence or the gossip that was floating around her. All the while, of course, she was suffering, and was never so glad to have an evening end. When she got home, she dismissed her maid, undressed herself, and crawled under the covers, where she cried herself to sleep. She had meant what she said to Mark: she would marry Tony, one way or another. But she had so hoped to marry the man she knew Tony could become.

Mark went home frustrated and furious. He had hardly needed to plant a spy in the house, had he? he asked himself sarcastically. Claudia herself was perfectly willing to tell him where things stood. While he had intended to provoke her by his use of his private information, it certainly had not been to a declaration. Although, now that he thought of it, it was his use of Jim's information that had gotten her to reveal the state of her heart. She was obviously determined to marry Ashford, no matter what kind of fool he was. He would have to do something—and soon—to prevent it.

9

Tony had intended to ignore the gossips and attend the Devonshire House rout. He knew Claudia was expecting him and he knew he should be there, showing his affection, so that she didn't suffer more from rumor than he did. But when the moment came, he couldn't do it. He couldn't face her again with empty pockets. He had looked desperately around his room and finally had sent his valet out with his second-best pair of boots and a gold watch that had belonged to his father. He had almost added the Ashford signet ring, but the act of pulling it off his finger brought back the day before Ned had died. His brother had been too weak to do it himself and had lifted his hand to Tony and whispered: "Take it now, Tony. It will be yours very soon anyway." He had protested, but Ned had just smiled and run his hand gently over his brother's curls as Tony lay his head on Ned's hand, trying to choke back the tears. He had already failed Ned miserably, but he would not sell the Ashford ring.

The boots and the watch fetched enough so that he could go back to 75 St. James and lay more money in the black. He had started with black, been lucky with it, and he was not going to desert it. He'd be faithful to one thing in his life, by God, even if it was only to the color of a card.

He started out low, being careful of his money, and when he lost on the first three deals, he still had enough to place a small bet on the fourth. He won. And kept on winning. By the end of the evening he had recouped almost three hundred guineas of Claudia's money. His step on the stairs to his lodgings was a lot lighter coming in than it had been going out. He fell into his bed exhausted and didn't wake up until the next afternoon.

He didn't call on Claudia, but sent her a small bouquet of flowers, promising to see her at the Ferrars', and asking her to save him a waltz. He was tempted to pay off a few creditors, but decided that he would wait. He wanted to show Claudia the money he'd won and assure her that all he needed was another three hundred. The last loan. And this time he would pay off his debts, every last one of them. And then ask Claudia to marry him.

He arrived early at the Ferrars' dinner dance, creating a minor storm of gossip. By now, of course, it was known he had won the night before, so no one was surprised that he was present and at his most charming.

"Not that he ever lets on when he is losing," said Lord Burleigh to his host. "I've never seen anyone cooler than Ashford."

When Claudia arrived, Tony approached her immediately. He had decided to act as though nothing had happened. She undoubtedly had heard gossip, but he wanted to explain himself in the privacy of her drawing room, not at a crowded dinner dance.

Their waltz was something of a disappointment. Although Tony was at his most charming, it felt like a brittle charm to his partner. And all the while they danced, Claudia could not help wondering whether Tony would admit his failure to her.

She had been claimed for supper and was already seated when she saw Tony escort Lady Joanna Barrand in. They were old friends from childhood, Claudia knew, and closer in age than she and Tony. Suddenly she felt her spirits sink. Perhaps affectionate friendship would not be enough for her. Tony was not treating Joanna any differently than he treated Claudia. Although at least she had Tony's kisses, after all.

Tony was not having as comfortable a supper as it appeared. He was trying to keep his mind off Claudia and on

Joanna, but was finding it difficult, and Joanna was not making it any easier. Oh, she was chatting away with him, but he could feel a certain coolness in the air. She would have heard the gossip too, and probably, like everyone else, saw him as a fortune hunter. He cared a great deal about what Joanna thought of him, for she was connected so closely to childhood and Ned in his mind. At some point he would have to reassure her that he did care about Lady Fairhaven, above and beyond her money.

Joanna thought she had been unhappy at the beginning of the Season when Tony's interest in Lady Fairhaven had first become evident. She had watched them closely, wondering why she was tormenting herself, but wanting some sign that Tony cared about the lady as well as her fortune.

Of course, when she saw them on the dance floor or seeking "fresh air," she decided, to Tony's credit, he seemed to have some genuine feeling for Lady Fairhaven. But aside from her relief that her old friend's integrity was more or less intact, it did not make her feel any better.

She was the world's biggest fool, she decided. She had loved Tony Varden since she was a young girl. When Ned died, she had been ashamed that her real grief was mixed with hope that the loss of his brother might bring them closer, might reshape the habits and patterns of old friendship. But Tony had never sought comfort from her. Instead, he had sought it at 75 St. James Street. And then in the arms of Lady Fairhaven. The one thing Joanna could be thankful for was that no one had ever guessed her secret.

Tony's most recent behavior had appalled her. If gossips were correct, he had borrowed a tidy sum from Claudia and immediately thrown it away on Rouge et Noir. And here he was, acting as if nothing had happened. How could she respect, much less love, such a man?

At the end of the evening, Tony asked Claudia if he might escort her home. She knew they had to have it out sometime, and so she agreed. The ride home was made in uncomfortable silence, now that there were no social forms to ease their way.

The butler opened the door for them and motioned to Jim to take their wraps.

"Please bring a decanter of brandy to the library, Dawson."

"Yes, my lady."

"Will you join me, Tony?" asked Claudia, not waiting for an answer and proceeding down the hall to the library. Tony followed, aware that she had chosen a rather formal room for their confrontation, for that was what he expected this to be.

Claudia was shaking with both anger and nerves. Here she was, deeply in love with a man who was on the brink of disaster. She had been able to dismiss Tony's gambling as a result of his grief and desperation. But he had made her a promise and not kept his word. She knew of too many men who made a life of broken promises over gambling or drinking. She wanted to save Tony from that, but she was not about to sacrifice herself in the process.

"Please close the door, Tony," she said, and turned to face him.

He looked like a shamefaced boy for one unguarded moment, and this time it did not draw her sympathy but her anger. At some point that boy had to grow up. It was high time.

"I have heard the gossip, Tony. In fact, I have had to put up with Lord Fairhaven warning me that everyone knows you have borrowed money from me and gambled it away. Can you explain?"

Tony was taken aback. He had never seen Claudia angry, nor expected to face more than disappointment. All his *savoir faire* deserted him, and unfortunately he looked even more boyish as he attempted an explanation. Reaching into his pocket, he pulled out the three hundred-pound notes and held them out.

"I did lose the other night, Claudia, but I won back half of it."

"But you did not pay off any of your debts as you promised."

"Well . . . no . . . you see, I was hoping to double what you had given me and pay you back as well."

"And now?"

"I know this will sound outrageous . . . but I was hoping you could lend me more. Only three hundred this time," he rushed to point out before she could open her mouth.

Neither heard the door click behind them or noticed Dawson standing there with the brandy.

"You are a fool indeed if you think I will give you a penny more of my money, Lord Ashford," said Claudia, furious at his effrontery.

Dawson cleared his throat. "The brandy, my lady."

Claudia blushed and Tony turned his back to the butler, walking over to the window.

"Set it down, Dawson. And you may retire."

"Thank you, my lady."

Tony turned around and looked Claudia in the eye. "I understand completely, Lady Fairhaven. I am sure you wish me in Jericho right now. I promise I will not bother you again. I cannot spare you the gossip, but it will die down, I assure you."

There was no trace of the bewildered boy in Tony's eyes. They were a man's eyes, bleak and despairing, but at least facing things as they were.

"Don't leave, Tony," said Claudia softly as he turned to go.

"I am sure I have hurt you, Claudia, and I wouldn't have done that for the world. I do have a great affection for you. I want you to know that. And we both have felt the attraction between us. But I also need your money. God help me," he groaned, "I never thought I would end up the rankest fortune hunter. But at least I can leave you alone from now on."

"So that I can fall prey to a fortune hunter who doesn't care about me? Or even desire me?" asked Claudia with a crooked smile. "Someone like Mark Halesworth?"

"Mark Halesworth! God forbid!"

"You know," said Claudia, pointing at the portrait of her

husband, "I almost think that Justin made his will in such a way that the title and fortune might be brought together. He may have meant well, but I could never marry Mark."

"I hope not, Claudia. Even I would be better than Fairhaven."

"Much better, Tony," she agreed.

"What are you saying, Claudia?"

"I think I am going to ask you to marry me, Tony."

"You are mad!"

"No. I am quite sane and serious. But there is a condition."

"Yes?"

"You would have to give up gambling. I will not marry someone I cannot trust."

"And could you trust me now, if I made you another promise?"

"I think so. Because if you marry me, you would have no more reason to return to the tables. As my husband, you will have all the money you need to restore Ashford and take care of your mother. But if you break *this* promise, Tony, I will break our engagement. I promise you that as faithfully as I promise my love."

Tony didn't move. He couldn't. He knew he should do something. What? Sweep her into his arms and rain kisses on her face to thank her? It would have felt despicable to take advantage of such generosity. No, he would begin this betrothal honestly, or not at all.

He put his hands on her shoulders and looked down into her eyes. "Claudia, I will make that promise. And not only for Ashford, although that is part of it. I won't begin this with a lie. Nor can I even begin to thank you right now. But I can tell you that I care for you very much and that I find it difficult at this moment to resist your lips. But I want to prove these things to you slowly, day by day."

"Then your answer is yes?"

"My answer is yes."

Claudia let out a long breath. "That was very unwomanly of me to propose, I know . . ."

"I am glad you did. I don't know when I would have had the courage. But I must go, or I will break my first promise and have to kiss you."

"I wouldn't mind that broken promise, Tony," Claudia whispered.

"I know, my dear, but first I need to redeem the other." Tony squeezed her hands and turned to go.

"Wait, my dear. You have forgotten something." Claudia walked over to her husband's desk and, opening the drawer, took out three hundred pounds.

Tony blushed. "I hate to take this."

"But you must."

"Unfortunately I must," he admitted. "I will redeem my vowels tonight."

"You may tell all your creditors that they will be fully paid over the next two weeks."

"Thank you, Claudia."

"Good night, Tony," she said, smiling at him.

"I will call on you tomorrow. Good night, my lady," he added, caressing her with his voice.

10

After Tony had gone, Claudia perched on the arm of the sofa and looked up at her husband's likeness.

"I am sorry to have to disappoint you, Justin. But I know that Tony and I are well matched." She smiled up as though Justin had answered her. "Yes, yes, there is a slight difference in our ages and he needs my money—but with all that, there is a chance for real love, I think. It seems I am as much a gambler as Tony, for I am willing to take my chances on that. And I could never have married Mark, my dear."

"I am very sorry to hear that, Claudia," said a voice behind her.

Claudia nearly fell off the sofa. "What are you doing here at this hour, Mark? Who let you in?" She was so furious at having her privacy violated that she didn't even care what he had overheard.

"I came at once when I heard Ashford had escorted you home. I was afraid you would succumb to his wheedling charm, and now I hear that you have. James let me in."

"Well, I will have to speak with James in the morning," replied Claudia, getting up and walking to the door.

Mark blocked her way. "Oh, no, you are not leaving yet."

"Get out of my way, Mark, before I call for James and embarrass us both." Mark didn't move.

"Get *out* of my way," Claudia repeated.

"Get out of your way? When you have been in my way these past seventeen years! No, my lady, you are going to hear me out," said Mark, grabbing her by the shoulders and backing her toward the sofa. He gave one shove and Claudia sat down with a gasp.

"How dare you touch me like that! Justin would have horsewhipped you."

"Yes? Well, Justin is gone, although that was quite a touching monologue I overheard. And Justin was a fool."

"Justin's little finger was worth more than every bone in your body, sir!"

Mark kept talking as though he hadn't even heard her. As though, Claudia thought, she wasn't even there.

"First, he had to go and marry a seventeen-year-old. Every summer I would dread my visit, worrying that you would at last be increasing. And every summer my hopes would rise again. But then I'd spend the whole year worrying. Of course, after a few years it did seem unlikely, and then, just not possible. No way of knowing, of course, if it was you or Justin to blame, but it is usually the woman's fault, I understand," he added contemptuously. "Then when Justin died . . . Well, that was a wonderful day."

Claudia made a sound between a laugh and a sob, but Mark just went on as though he hadn't heard her.

"Until they read the will. Oh, yes, I got the title and the estate. They were entailed, he had no choice. But you . . . you got everything else, everything I'd worked for and waited for all those years."

"*Justin* had worked for it. And Justin gave you more than enough to support both the estate and yourself in style."

Mark looked down, and the hatred in his eyes frightened her so much that she sank back into the sofa.

"I think you are right about one thing, Claudia. I think Justin set up his will to bring us together. That way, I would have both the title and the fortune."

"But according to your reasoning, no heir."

"Who knows what might have happened, Claudia, who knows? But now it is too late. Or is it, my dear? Are you really going to marry that irresponsible boy, Cousin Claudia?"

"Lord Ashford is not a boy, Mark. He is a young man who temporarily caved in under tremendous pressure. He has convinced me that he is to be trusted and, more important, he cares about me. And I care for him. You care for no one but yourself. I always suspected it, but I never disillusioned Justin."

"How kind of you." Mark sat down next to her, and only with the greatest effort could Claudia keep herself from shrinking away from him.

"I was hoping Ashford would not redeem himself . . . or his vowels," added Mark with a humorless chuckle at his own pun. "But it seems he has."

"Yes. As of tonight, we are betrothed."

"And if you marry and should you conceive, then all that money is lost to me forever. I cannot let that happen."

"You can't do anything to stop it, Mark." Claudia started to get up. "Now please go."

Mark pushed her back down and pinned her to the sofa with his knee between her legs. He cradled her head in his hands and brought his face close, as though he were going to kiss her, but there was no warmth, no humanity, in his cold, shuttered stare. Suddenly, Claudia was very frightened again.

"There is one way to stop you from marrying Ashford, my dear."

Claudia froze as his thumbs moved gently on her throat, as though seeking her pulse, which, no doubt, was racing. But she would not give him the satisfaction of showing her fear.

"Let me go, Mark," she said as calmly as she could.

"Oh, no, I can't let you go and do something as foolish as marry Ashford instead of me," he whispered.

Claudia shrank even further back against the sofa, wondering whether he meant to ravish her in her own library. Her servants were all in bed, unlikely to hear her if she screamed. It was only when she felt his thumbs press on either side of her throat, first gently, then harder, that she began to realize that her life, not just her body, was in danger. But surely she thought, as she felt the pressure increase, so that the only sound she was aware of was the roaring of her own pulse in her ears, surely Mark would not really kill her . . . *Tony* . . . she thought. *Justin* . . . But neither could help her now. The roar became louder, and then there was only silence.

Mark looked at her limp body and then at his hands. He had never considered himself a violent man; in fact, for years he had been the epitome of self-control, but a cold rage had come over him when he had overheard Claudia's little speech to Justin. In some strange way, he felt perfectly justified in his action: the inheritance should have been his, was his, and he had no intention of losing it now. Ashford had been the last person seen with Claudia and he would have to make Tony Varden look like the murderer.

He got up and went to his cousin's desk and pulled every drawer open and scattered some of the contents on the floor. Then he rumpled the small Turkey carpet in front of the sofa and upended a delicately carved table his cousin had brought back from India.

Claudia lay as though she were asleep. "Too peaceful, my dear," he murmured. "No, I think you will be found on the floor, your gown torn a little, your hair pulled down." And he suited actions to words, finally lifting her body and dropping it on the rug, where it lay, arms and legs angled awkwardly.

"Ashford enters, asks for more money. You refuse it and tell him you won't see him again. He kills you quietly and skillfully, as a well-trained soldier might kill a *guerrillero*."

Mark's back was to the door and he was too involved to realize that it had opened. Jim, who had let Tony out and Mark in, had been standing sleepily in the front hall wondering when he could go to bed. Dawson had told him to see the mistress up to her room, but at this rate, she would be up all night and so would he. She was a kind woman, Lady Fairhaven, and he was sure if he looked in on her and asked if she needed anything, she would send him off to bed.

But Lady Fairhaven would never need anything again. Of that he was sure. And there was his real employer, opening drawers, disarranging rugs, and muttering something about Lord Ashford. Jim was not brilliant, but anyone could see what Fairhaven was up to. Lady Fairhaven had been alone when Ashford left, of that Jim was certain, for Tony had even asked him to look in on her. He would never have done that, were he her killer. No, Lord Fairhaven had killed her, and he, Jim, was a witness. Not only a witness but a spy, placed in the household by Fairhaven himself. And oh, God, if Fairhaven saw him now, he might not hesitate to kill again.

He pulled the door slowly and gently closed and tiptoed down the hall. His things? Forget them. Money? He had Fairhaven's vail, thank God, and a guinea from Ashford, who had been in a happy and generous mood when he left. That would keep him for a while. Right now, he had to get out of the house and lose himself somewhere in London.

11

When Lady Fairhaven's maid knocked on her door the next morning and got no response, she quietly stepped into the room, intending to draw the curtains back. Her mistress was not usually a late or heavy sleeper, but on those rare occasions when she slept in, she appreciated being awakened by the admission of sunlight. The abigail was very surprised to see that the bed had never been slept in.

She had no idea where her mistress might be, although for one minute Lord Ashford's face came to mind. But that was ridiculous. Lady Fairhaven would never have gone to his rooms alone, much less spent the night. When she got downstairs, she found the butler questioning the other servants about Jim. "He should have been on duty in the breakfast room an hour ago," said Mr. Dawson, with great annoyance.

"Well, I haven't seen him this morning," the housekeeper replied.

"Mr. Dawson."

"Yes, Mary?" said Dawson impatiently.

"Lady Fairhaven is not in her room—nor has she been there, from the looks of things."

The butler frowned. "Not in her room? She was with Lord Ashford in the library when I retired last night. Indeed, she sent me up to bed herself. Perhaps she fell asleep on the sofa?"

"Mr. Dawson!"

"Well, we all know what is going on there, Mary. He

might have stayed, um, very late. Although, I must say, when I walked in, the evening did not seem to be heading that way. I'll go down and see."

Dawson knocked softly on the library door and then opened it. At first, he could not take in what he saw. Lady Fairhaven lay there indeed, but not peacefully on the sofa. And how could a woman have spent the night on the floor in that odd position? he thought, his mind refusing to take in the reality of his mistress's dead body.

He leaned down and felt for her pulse. None. Gently running his hand down her face, he closed her eyes and tried to smooth back her hair. After adjusting her gown so it covered her legs, he straightened up and stood there in shock, looking around the room and registering the overturned table and the open drawers of the desk. He was finally drawn to the portrait of his late master, almost expecting Lord Fairhaven's eyes to turn accusingly on him. But they looked straight ahead, and Dawson would have sworn on his mother's life that his master's face had subtly changed. There was a look of tenderness in the eyes that seemed to be saying, "There is no need for sadness, for she has come home to me."

The butler shook his head to clear it of such foolish fancies, and closing the door behind him, went to face the other servants.

"No one is to go into the library until a constable has been here."

"A constable!" exclaimed the housekeeper.

"Yes, Mrs. Pitt. It seems . . . " Dawson cleared his throat. "It seems that Lady Fairhaven has been murdered."

While they were awaiting the arrival of the constable, Dawson questioned the rest of the servants. No, they had heard nothing, all having been in bed for hours on the third floor. William, who shared a room with Jim, said he had gone to sleep immediately and only upon getting up had he noticed that the other bed was empty.

The butler went up with him to inspect the room. "Is anything of his missing, William?"

"No, Mr. Dawson. It doesn't look like it to me," said William after a quick glance around the room.

When the constable arrived, he repeated many of the same questions and then closeted himself with the butler.

"Tell me everything you remember about last evening, Mr. Dawson."

"Lady Fairhaven returned home at about two a.m. She was accompanied by Lord Ashford."

"What do you know about Lord Ashford? Is he an old friend?"

"Not so much an old friend as a young . . . admirer," replied Dawson.

The constable lifted his eyebrows inquiringly and the butler continued.

"Lady Fairhaven had been seeing a lot of this young man and we all assumed that she might eventually marry him. Or at least, that is what it looked like until last night."

"What do you mean?"

"When they arrived, they went directly to the library and not the drawing room, where it is more comfortable, as though they had business in mind and not pleasure. And when I came in with a tray of brandy, they seemed to be arguing."

"About what?"

"Lady Fairhaven was refusing to lend the earl any more money."

"So she has lent him money in the past?"

"Well, the word is that Ashford is badly dipped. Owes the blacklegs and his tailor and chandler, among others."

"Did Lord Ashford seem angry?"

"More embarrassed, I would say. He turned away from me immediately."

"And your mistress?"

"My lady was a lovely woman. I have never heard her speak so sharply to anyone. But she was sharp last night."

"Is that all you know? That she wouldn't give him the money he needed? Did she refuse to see him again?"

"I don't know. I suppose she could have, but I didn't hear it. She sent me up to bed directly after I served the brandy."

"So there was no one else here besides Lord Ashford?"

"No, no, Jim was in the hall."

"Jim? I haven't met Jim."

"No, well, Jim is the new under-footman and I asked him to stay up and see Lord Ashford out and Lady Fairhaven up to her room. But he was gone this morning. Disappeared without even taking any of his things with him."

"There were no signs of foul play anywhere else?"

"What?"

"Blood or signs of struggle?"

"No, no. You don't think someone killed Jim too?"

"It is a possibility to consider. But from what I see, no. It may be he had a very good reason to leave."

Dawson looked puzzled.

"Either he killed Lady Fairhaven, or he saw who did."

12

By noon, most of society was buzzing about the death of Lady Fairhaven. Some had heard that Lord Ashford had been the last to see her alive and gave knowing looks to one another. Others heard that a new footman had disappeared. And bets were being laid at Brooks as to who was the more likely suspect. The odds were clearly in favor of Tony Varden.

Tony himself had heard nothing yet. He had been tempted to go straight to St. James Street and pay off his debts, but then thought better of it. He wasn't sure he could trust himself, so he just went home. His valet was already in bed, and Tony undressed himself and fell asleep immediately, free for the first time in weeks of nagging worries and guilt and shame. He would *not* gamble again and he would make Claudia the loving husband she deserved. The fact that he wasn't in love with her didn't seem to matter to her, and he had hope that his own feelings would deepen over time.

He slept late and was awakened by his valet shaking his shoulder and saying in a worried voice: "Wake up, my lord, there is a Runner here to see you."

As he climbed up from the depths of sleep, he had an odd fantasy of a young man, looking like a figure from the Greek games, waiting to meet him. Then it penetrated. "Oh, God, it must be the tailor. He's laid charges and they are going to take me off to the Marshalsea. Well, thank God, I can pay them.

Tony threw on his dressing gown, and fumbling through his clothes, pulled out the money Claudia had given him.

The Runner was standing by the door inspecting a Stubbs print on the wall. He was an unprepossessing figure of a man, thought Tony. Not at all what you would expect a thief-taker to look like.

"You are come from Grants, I presume?" Tony asked with his most charming smile.

The Runner turned and looked blankly at him.

"Or McLean? Well, no matter," said Tony. "You can tell whoever it is to send someone over. I can pay every penny I owe." He waved a fistful of notes in the air.

"Lord Ashford?" inquired the Runner.

"Yes," said Tony impatiently. Lord, but the man's face was nondescript and expressionless.

"I am Gideon Naylor. You are under a misapprehension about the reason for my visit."

"I am?"

"Yes. I am not here to arrest you for debt."

"Well, thank God for that," Tony replied with a smile. "How can I help you, then?"

"You seem to have a sheaf of notes there. May I ask how you came by them?"

Tony frowned. "What is this? Has there been a robbery in the neighborhood? Have you come to arrest me for theft?" he added sarcastically.

"There appears to have been a theft, my lord. But it is on a far more serious matter that I have come. I am investigating the murder of Lady Claudia Fairhaven."

Tony looked blankly at Naylor. "Claudia? Why, Claudia can't be dead. I only saw her last night. Well, actually, early this morning. This is some sort of bad joke, isn't it?" continued Tony, his voice shaking with shock and anger.

"I am afraid it is no joke, my lord. Lady Fairhaven was found dead on the library floor this morning by her butler. And according to Mr. Dawson, you were the last person to have seen or spoken with her."

Tony sat down suddenly on one of the chairs around his

table. "No," he whispered. He raised his eyes to Naylor pleadingly. "Tell me it is not true."

Naylor just stared back, his face expressionless.

"How . . . how was she killed?"

"The coroner has not come to any conclusions yet, my lord."

"Please God it was quick," murmured Tony.

"The drawers in her late husband's desk were pulled out, my lord, and appear to have been rifled. May I ask where you got that money?"

"What? You mean you think it was an attempted robbery?"

"Not *attempted*, Lord Ashford. Where did the money come from?"

The man was persistent, Tony had to give him that. Maybe he just wore suspects down, rather than threatening them.

"I won some of it the night before last and the rest Claudia—Lady Fairhaven—gave me last night."

The Runner pulled out a small notebook and pencil. "Where did you win, my lord, and how much?"

Tony hesitated, and then said, "I can't tell you."

"Oh, come, my lord, this is a murder investigation. I can easily find out what hells you frequent, but if you tell me, it will go quicker."

"Seventy-five St. James Street. You can ask one of the blacklegs. Boniface. He'll vouch for me."

"And who will vouch for the rest of the money?"

"Why, Claudia, of course," Tony answered without thinking, and then, realizing that Claudia would never speak for him or anyone else again, he buried his face in his hands and wept.

Naylor just waited quietly until Tony's shoulders were still.

"Lady Fairhaven's butler is willing to testify that he heard her very angrily refuse to give you another penny."

Tony raised his face, outraged. "Why, that is not true," he started to protest angrily, and then stopped. He took a deep breath, and running his hand over his face, continued. "Dawson probably did hear Lady Fairhaven say that. I remember when he came in with the brandy we were in the middle of a disagreement. But he left before our conversation concluded."

"Conversation or quarrel, my lord?"

"Disagreement, quarrel, what does it matter? We said good-night on the best of terms. In fact, we were unofficially betrothed," said Tony bleakly.

"And we only have your word for it."

Tony drew himself up and said haughtily: "The word of a Varden is not given lightly, I assure you, Mr. Naylor."

"Be that as it may, I am afraid I must arrest you for the murder of Lady Claudia Fairhaven."

"What! You must be out of your mind!"

"Not at all, my lord. You were the last person to have been seen with Lady Fairhaven. You were overheard quarreling with her over money. And you now have quite a bit of money. You were a soldier on the Peninsula, I believe?"

"Yes, and what has that got to do with anything?"

"Although the coroner has not made his final report, he does have some suspicions. The only signs of violence were thumbprints on both sides of Lady Fairhaven's throat. He suspects pressure on the carotid arteries, my lord, a very quick and silent way of killing that a seasoned soldier like yourself might know."

Tony blanched. "So might anyone else. A burglar. Have you thought of that? She may have been surprised by a common thief."

"It would be rare for our common thief to kill so expertly. Bludgeoning is more a burglar's style."

Tony looked blankly down at his hands and then up at Naylor. "I swear that I didn't kill Lady Fairhaven, Naylor. But I am glad whoever did chose that method. It would have been swift and painless and she wouldn't have suffered. May I see her?"

"You will be in Newgate within the half hour, my lord."

"You are making a terrible mistake, Naylor. And letting

the real murderer get away. But short of knocking you down and making myself look even more guilty, I suppose I have no choice," said Tony with painful irony.

"I would not be so easily overcome, my lord," said Naylor with a quick smile.

"No? You certainly don't look threatening."

"I was a soldier in the Forty-seventh Foot before I became a Runner, my lord. And I have found that a mild appearance often works as well as a threatening one." Naylor cleared his throat. "I must ask you to get dressed and come with me, Lord Ashford."

Tony nodded and pushed his chair back. "But before you do," continued Naylor, "you will give me the money."

Tony looked down at the sheaf of notes. It was all he had, and the only thing that stood between him and a common cell at Newgate.

"Half of this is mine, Naylor. Well, all of it, since Claudia did give it to me. Of course, my creditors would say none of it is," he added with a poor attempt at humor.

"Be that as it may, it is evidence. After I've verified your story, I'll see what I can do about getting some of it back to you."

Tony's hand rested a moment on top of the money, and then, calling his valet, he went to get dressed.

"John, you are going to have to go to the pawnbroker's again, but with what, God knows."

"Your ring, my lord?"

"No, I can't sell it, even if I starve. No, take my best boots and a few shirts. Here, here are some books, too. That should keep me for a day or two. And I most certainly will be out by then. This whole charge is ridiculous and will soon be proved so."

13

The trip to Newgate was made in silence. Gideon Naylor sat opposite his prisoner in a hansom cab and observed him carefully. Ashford was a handsome young man, that was true enough, he thought, with his dark blond curls and brown eyes. He was sure that those eyes could look teasing or soulfully romantic, depending upon his lordship's mood and purpose. Right now, they were focused on his lordship's hands. He seemed to be looking at his signet ring and fingering it, as though to reassure himself that he was still Anthony Varden, Lord Ashford.

Lady Fairhaven had been married off by her parents to an older man. Her servants had assured Naylor that it had been a very happy marriage. Nevertheless, Gideon was sure that a young, handsome man like Ashford could easily have captured the widow's heart. And her fortune. Ashford was desperate, from what he had found out, and desperation could drive a man to deeds he would otherwise have been incapable of.

On the other hand, there was that missing footman, who was new in the household and therefore an unknown quantity. The butler indicated that Jim had seemingly been devoted to his new mistress. But a few weeks was a short time to develop loyalty.

And there was also the lady's cousin by marriage to consider. Gideon had met him briefly at the house. He had appeared to be as shocked as Varden at the news, but Gideon was making no final assumptions about the case yet. Ashford was clearly the prime suspect: he had motive, he was the last person to see Lady Fairhaven alive, and he had her money. True, he seemed genuinely distraught, but then many a criminal regretted this sort of crime, one committed in the passion of the moment. One the criminal would never have thought himself capable of. And one that occurred all too often.

When they reached the prison, Naylor, moved by a moment of compassion that surprised him, asked Lord Ashford if he had any money.

Tony looked up blankly. He was so dazed by the events of the morning that he hadn't even realized they'd arrived.

"A shilling or two, Naylor. You've kindly relieved me of the rest of my money. But my valet is out selling some things, so I should have money by this evening."

"Well, until he gets here, my lord, you will be in the felons' court. You'll be able to afford a bed and some food, at least. And if your valet can get enough, they will let you a private room. Your friends can visit and bring you food and whatever else you need."

"Friends? All my close friends are in the army, Naylor. Back here . . . well, Lady Fairhaven was my friend. And Joanna," he added. "The rest are only gaming companions, hardly the sort to concern themselves with my fate."

Naylor opened the cab door and motioned Tony down. The prison, a long brick building, looked surprisingly new to Tony, considering there had been a jail there for five hundred years. Then he remembered: the original Newgate had been burned down in the Gordon riots and then rebuilt.

They were admitted by a short, squat man who reminded Tony of a frog, who handed them over to the turnkey. As they walked toward the felons' court, the stench, which had been faint at the door, became overpowering and Tony gagged as bile rose in his throat. It was only through sheer will power that he kept himself from vomiting.

"'Ere we are, my lord," said the turnkey, letting Tony into the felons' quadrangle. Tony took a few steps and then turned to Naylor, saying desperately: "I can't stay here,

Naylor. I didn't kill Lady Fairhaven. You must believe me."

"Believe you or no, my lord, first must come a magistrates' hearing. That will decide whether there is enough evidence against you to keep you for trial. Right now, however, there is enough evidence for arrest. But I will see that your man gets in easily."

And then Naylor was gone with the turnkey, and Tony felt himself pressed in on either side by fellow prisoners, some of whom took notice of him only to push or shove him out of their way, others who ignored him. All of them were pale, filthy, and stinking. He made his way slowly to the far end of the quadrangle, hoping for a corner in which to take a breath. He finally reached the wall and pressed himself back against it, as though if he leaned hard enough he would pass through and be out on the street and free.

The man next to him, a tall, cadaverous-looking fellow, poked him in the ribs.

"Yer first time, eh, guv? Ye look loike yere about ready to cast up yere accounts. Just don't do it on me," he joked. "Wot you in for?"

Tony looked at him blankly.

"Wot old Naylor catch you doin'? A swell loike you is usually over on the debtors' side."

"Murder. I am in for murder."

"So ham Oi, guv, so ham Oi."

Tony slid sideways along the wall.

"No need to be a shrinking violet, guv. Oi ain't no murderer."

"Neither am I," whispered Tony.

"Oi did it in self-defense. Hif Oi 'adn't killed Matt Farnley, 'e would 'ave surely killed me. Oi owed 'im that much blunt, ye see, and when 'e came after me, well, wot's a bloke to do, eh? Ye got any blunt, guv?"

"A few shillings."

"Well, hif Oi was you, Oi would 'and some of those there shillings right over to me, Oi would. A swell gent loike yereself ain't goin' to be too popular 'ere. On the other 'and," the man continued with a rough nudge in Tony's ribs, "ye might be more popular with some than you would prefer." The man leered and winked. "Anyways, Oi can provide ye with protection."

Tony hated to give up any money, but what choice had he? Please God, John would come soon, and at least he could get himself a private room. In hell, it was true, but at least he wouldn't fear for his life. He drew out five shillings.

"Fanks, guv. That'll keep yer safe for today, hat least." And Tony's protector moved off, leaving him against the wall, waiting for the scene in front of him to make sense, for the crowd to separate out into recognizable individuals, for himself to take in the fact that Anthony Varden, Lord Ashford, was now considered a common felon. Or perhaps an uncommon felon, he thought ironically. He took a deep breath, which was a mistake, and he finally and painfully vomited against the wall, adding one more foul smell to the fetid air.

14

Joanna had been sleeping late for the past few weeks, which was unusual for her. She was normally an early riser and often went for an early-morning ride, before the park was crowded. She would not admit that her tiredness was due to her despair over Tony and Lady Fairhaven. Her excuse to herself was that she had been uncommonly active this past fortnight, although in truth she had attended no more social functions than usual.

Her parents were still at the breakfast table when she finally came down, and seemed rather subdued. She accepted a plate from the footman and poured her own cup of tea, as was her habit.

"Thank you, Matthew. Good morning, *mes parents*," she said with a smile.

"Good morning, dear," her mother replied. "I trust you slept well."

"Why yes, Mother, and later again than usual, as you can see."

Her father put his newspaper down, and looking meaningfully over at his wife, said: "I thought we agreed you would tell her, Sylvia."

"Tell me what, Father?"

Lady Barrand took a deep breath. "Something terrible has happened, Joanna. Tony Varden . . ."

Joanna's face turned pale. "Tell me immediately, Mother. Is Tony injured? Dead? Was he killed in some hell in a fight over cards?"

The look of pain in her daughter's eyes frightened Lady

Barrand. She had always suspected that Joanna was more than half in love with their handsome young neighbor, but she had hoped it wasn't so, especially when Tony, inheriting such a burden, turned to cards and a rich widow as a solution. Joanna had hidden her feelings very well. On the one hand, this was a good thing, for no gossip had ever surfaced about her and Tony. On the other, she had also kept her feelings from her parents, and Lady Barrand had always respected her daughter's privacy. She had wanted to offer comfort for weeks, but it had been impossible until now.

"No, no, Joanna. But it is almost worse than that."

Joanna sighed with relief. To her, nothing could be worse. Even knowing Tony was likely to marry Lady Fairhaven would be nothing compared to losing him altogether. A world without Tony in it somewhere was not a world worth living in.

"What your mother is trying to tell you, Joanna, is that Lady Fairhaven was murdered early this morning, and Tony has been arrested for the crime."

Joanna dropped her fork, which clattered against her plate. The sound was very loud and seemed to go on forever. Then she found her voice.

"Tony a murderer? That is ridiculous. How on earth could they have arrested him?"

"Evidently he was the last person to be seen with her. The butler overheard them quarreling about money before he was sent up to bed. And in the morning, when the servants came down, they found their mistress on the library floor, with things in disarray around her."

"It was obviously a burglary, then," protested Joanna.

"I am sure there are other details we are not yet aware of, my dear," said her mother.

"But, Mother, you cannot believe this! You both *know* Tony."

"I would never have believed it before. But Tony was desperate, you know. Deeply in debt and with Ashford depending upon him."

"And gaming is like a fever, Joanna," said her father. "It

takes control of a man. If Lady Fairhaven refused him money . . . ?"

"I don't care how desperate Tony was, he could never kill anyone, especially a woman he cared about."

"Joanna, he *has* killed, many times, one would assume. After all, he has been a soldier for years."

"But that is different, Father."

"It is different, but the experience can harden a man."

"Not enough to kill a woman he . . . loved."

"But do you think he was really in love with Lady Fairhaven, dear?" asked Lady Barrand. "Isn't it rather unlikely? She was older than he, after all."

"Only by five years, Mother. And she is—was—a very attractive woman. And from all I knew of her, a kind woman. I think Tony cared a lot about her."

"Well, be that as it may, at least you know, and you are prepared for all the gossip," said her father, pushing back from the table to signal the conversation was at an end. "What are your plans for the day, Joanna?"

"I am promised to go shopping and to Gunter's with Amelia Grant."

"Good," said her mother. "I think if you keep busy today, you will feel better. And who knows, Joanna, Tony may be released right after the hearing."

Joanna nodded and sat staring at her plate. She had no appetite now, although she did feel uncommonly thirsty, and gulped down a second cup of tea. Thank goodness she was past the age when her parents kept close tabs on her. As long as she had her abigail with her, they didn't question her comings and goings much. Today she was committed, but tomorrow she intended to visit Newgate and talk to Tony. She wanted to hear his side of the story face-to-face.

15

When John had not arrived by the time the prisoners were served their meager supper, Tony realized he was going to be spending the night in the main quadrangle. He paid a few more shillings for an extra bowl of soup and a cup of ale. Despite the smells, he was surprised to find he was still hungry and was just regretting his payment to his cadaverous protector when he felt himself being jostled on either side and a hand reaching into his coat. As he yelled and pulled away, his "friend" grabbed the two thieves and knocked their heads together. "This one's mine," he told them. "So get ye off." As the two slunk away, Tony stammered out a thank-you to his rescuer. "No need, guv. Ye paid fer hit."

Later, when Tony had stretched out on a low pallet and pulled a moth-eaten blanket over himself, both of which had cost him more money, he was suddenly aware that someone was running a hand over his hair and tracing the outline of his ear. He tried to pretend he was asleep, but couldn't help shivering as a voice whispered in his ear: "Yer 'air shines like a new guinea, lad. Move over and I'll show ye 'ow good ye can feel with Jem as yer mate."

The words were sweet enough, but the tone was hard and brooked no denial. Tony was just getting ready to send his elbow back into the man's stomach when he felt the weight lifted off him.

"Oi already told ye, Jem, 'e's off-limits fer tonight. Now find someone else."

"Aw right, Bill, aw right."

Tony could have wept with relief until Bill crawled in next to him.

"I thank you for your help, Bill, but what are you doing in my cot?"

"Why, that's part of my protective service, guv. Hif yer known to be mine, then no one else will go after ye."

"How much will it take to have you find another bed?"

"Oh, Oi can't do that. But another few shillings, and Oi won't do nuffink more than sleep 'ere."

Tony reached into his pocket. "Done."

"Fanks, guv."

Tony shrank to the edge of the pallet, balanced precariously on the edge as Bill pulled closer and wrapped his arms around him. He lay awake and vigilant, waiting for his companion to make a move. But very soon Bill was asleep, breathing softly, hand clasped around Tony's as though they were children taking shelter from the cold. *At least, I am safe until morning,* Tony thought. *Please God, let John come early,* and he drifted off to sleep.

The next morning, Bill was gone and Tony awoke with a pounding headache. He had not slept well, but had kept waking up to the varied sounds of the prison: a fight breaking out, one man's taking pleasure with another, and men calling out in their sleep.

How was he to endure another day of this? He sat on the edge of his cot, head buried in his hands, and thought that even Spain had been better than this, or at least, no worse. Surely no one could really believe he was a murderer? If Ned were alive, he'd tell them. He'd have gotten Tony out within an hour. But, of course, if Ned were alive, he wouldn't be here at all. He'd be back in his tent in Spain rather than rotting in Newgate. He wouldn't be the goddamned Earl of Ashford. He wouldn't be responsible for the estate. He would never have had to court Lady Claudia Fairhaven.

But when he thought of Claudia, all he could think of was their first meeting, when each had felt an instant sympathy with the other. He had not wooed her only for her money. He had cared for Claudia very much. He just hadn't loved her. That was his only crime. He knew she had loved him and he had taken advantage of her affection. But even that wasn't true. He had been honest about himself. And who was to say he wouldn't have come to love her? For Claudia, who was lovely and generous and sympathetic, deserved to be loved in return. Instead, she had been murdered. He wanted to cry for her again, but he couldn't. Not here.

Someone was calling his name. It was the turnkey, telling him that John had arrived. Thank God, he would at least have a private room for the night.

The expression on John's face almost made Tony laugh. He looked down at his rumpled clothes and rubbed a hand over his unshaven chin. "I know you are horrified, John, but there was not much I could do about it. Were you able to sell anything?"

"Yes, my lord. I got five guineas for the boots and two shirts and your maroon superfine."

"Good man," said Tony, with a broad smile. He felt as much relief as if John had brought enough to clear the estate. "That will buy me a private room for a while. Speaking of privacy," said Tony, addressing the turnkey, "can I have a few minutes alone with my valet? I promise you he has not come to help me escape," he added jokingly.

"All right, my lord, I can take you to the visitors' room."

When the turnkey had closed the door to the small chamber, Tony motioned his valet to sit down.

"John, I did not kill Lady Fairhaven."

His valet jumped out of his seat. "Of course not, my lord. As though you would think that I could entertain such a suspicion."

"Sit down, sit down. The point I am trying to make is that if I did not kill her, then someone else *did*. And that someone is still at large."

"I had not thought of that, my lord."

"Now, I was supposedly the last person to see her alive.

But what of her new footman, Jim? He let me out and he has disappeared. Perhaps he did it—for the money."

"Or it could have been an intruder, my lord."

"But if it were a burglar, then where is Jim?"

"Run away, my lord. Or perhaps dead?" John offered tentatively.

"Hmmm. I think a burglar is the weakest possibility. No, I think Jim is the stronger one. Not, of course, that I can do anything about it while I am in here," added Tony hopelessly.

"I heard the hearing is set for the day after tomorrow."

"Another two days here. I don't think I can stand it. You'll have to sell another jacket and two shirts. I need every shilling I can get."

"I'll be back with more money tomorrow, my lord."

"And John." John looked expectantly at his employer. "Thank you for believing in me."

The morning went excruciatingly slowly after John left. Here and there in the corners were groups of men with dice or tattered decks of cards. Tony could have joined them, but had no desire to. Whatever fire had fueled his obsession was banked for now, perhaps completely extinguished by the humiliation of asking Claudia for more money and then the realization that in some way, his gambling might have led to her death. Perhaps Jim had seen the rest of the money in the desk drawer. Perhaps someone else had known he had asked her for a loan.... There was no logic to his feeling of guilt. He hadn't loved Claudia the way she deserved to be loved, he had involved her in his financial difficulties, he had disappointed her, and she was dead. Had he not been frequenting St. James Street, maybe none of this would have happened. At any rate, he couldn't imagine ever wagering on anything again, even for a penny a point on a game of whist.

He had paid the turnkey for a room, and at last, in early afternoon, he was given a small cubicle off the main quadrangle. It wasn't much, but it was a hundred times better than living in the middle of a crowd of felons. The pallet was relatively clean and comfortable and there was a small deal table and chair and even a chamberpot. Granted, the pot didn't look as if it had ever been scrubbed, but it was empty and gave him privacy.

"Candles and plate cost half a guinea, my lord," said the turnkey as Tony inspected the three candleholders, which held only stubs. "A lantern is more."

Tony handed over the money with an unamused laugh. "You do well for yourself. Does the prison supply anything but bread and gruel?"

"Not much, my lord, not much," replied the man with a grin, and left Tony to himself.

He spent what felt like hours going over the past months since Ned's death. What could he have done differently? He wasn't his brother, that was certain. He hadn't been raised to the title, nor had he the temperament for the responsibilities. It now appeared ludicrous to him, however, that he had thought a few good nights at the tables would resolve all his problems. But at the time, the slow, methodical, painful way Ned had chosen had seemed the ridiculous solution. He had been twisting and turning his signet ring while he sat there remembering, and now he pulled it off and looked at it. "I don't deserve this, Ned," he whispered. "You should have lived and I been the one to die in Spain. God got it all wrong, Ned, all wrong. But I swear," declared Tony, pushing the ring back on his finger, "that I will do better. But, oh, God, I wish you were here to help me." It seemed to Tony that his brother was very close at that moment, watching, listening, and the sense of his presence and the kaleidoscope of memories that was going through his head broke through, at long last, the barrier he had erected against his grief. He turned his head to the wall, and burying his face in his pillow, wept from a place so deep that he thought he might retch his insides out. He cried for Ned, gone away too early, for his mother and Charlotte, and finally for Claudia, his good friend. And then, at long last, he slept.

16

He was shaken awake a few hours later by the gatesman.

"Wake up, my lord. You have another visitor."

"What?" mumbled Tony, sitting up and rubbing his swollen eyes.

"But you don't look half ready to see this one, guv. I can send a basin of water and a towel for ten shillings, hif you wish."

"Is my valet back?"

"Oh, no. This time it is a young woman. Or a lady, I should say. She calls herself Lady Joanna Barrand."

"Joanna! She shouldn't be here. Send her away immediately."

"I told her as how this was no place for a gentlewoman. But she did bring an abigail with her. And she insisted I tell you she was here."

"Oh, God," groaned Tony. "I can't see her like this."

The gatesman put out his hand.

"All right, all right. Bring me the water and towel, and I'll see her for a minute or two."

The water wasn't clean, nor was the towel, but then nothing was in this dreadful place. Tony did the best he could and smoothed his hair and brushed off his trousers and shirt and then followed the gatesman out to the visitors' room.

Joanna had been pacing the small room while her abigail sat stiffly in a chair with her handkerchief held to her nose. Although the smell of the prison was fainter here, it had permeated the walls enough to make both women feel queasy.

When she heard footsteps, Joanna turned and watched Tony and his guard walk down the corridor. She had never seen Tony look so bad, not even when Ned was dying. His clothes were wrinkled and dirty, he was unshaven, and his eyes looked as if he had been up for three days straight. His usually light athletic step had become heavy. Another day or two, thought Joanna in horror, and he would be shuffling.

He stopped at the door and the gatesman almost had to push him in.

"I'll give you some privacy, my lord, but remember, I am right outside the door," the guard said, and closed it behind him.

"Joanna, you shouldn't be here!" Tony protested in a hoarse voice.

Joanna had decided that a matter-of-fact approach rather than sympathy would save them both from embarrassment.

"Of course I would come, Tony. You are one of my oldest friends."

"Please sit down, then, Joanna."

Joanna sat and signaled to her abigail with her eyes. Sally rose and stood by the barred window, giving them the illusion of privacy.

Tony stood for a moment or two, and then seated himself into the chair opposite.

"What are you doing here, Jo? I can't believe your parents would have allowed it."

"They don't know I am here," she admitted. "They think I am out shopping. But I couldn't stand the rumors. I wanted to talk to you myself and see if there was anything I could do."

"And what are the rumors? No, don't tell me," Tony continued. "I can guess. The heartless and desperate young suitor of an older woman kills her in a moment of anger when she refuses him money to pay his debts."

"Something like that," Joanna said. "But how anyone could believe it . . . "

"Oh, I don't know, Jo. It is so close to the truth, why wouldn't they?" Tony responded wearily.

"But you didn't kill her, Tony."

"No," he replied, looking directly into her eyes. "No, I didn't kill her. But somehow I feel I may as well have been the one to put my hands around her neck. I feel responsible, Jo. I *was* desperate. I did borrow from her and she did at first refuse to give me more money. The butler heard that much before going to bed. But what he didn't hear was the rest of our conversation. I convinced her that I was sincere in my determination to stop gaming, and that I cared for her. By the time I left, we were unofficially betrothed. And she had given me the money that incriminated me."

"Did you love her, Tony?" Joanna asked, without really thinking. She *had* to know.

"We were good friends, Joanna. Like you and I. There was an instant sympathy between us. But Claudia knew how I felt about her. And I knew how she felt about me. She loved me, Jo. But I swear I was honest with her, and was sure that our marriage had every chance of becoming a very happy one, despite my motivation."

"To save Ashford?"

"Yes. What other way was there? And I thought it was not such a bad thing I was doing after all. I mean, most of the marriages we know are founded on less than friendship. And I think Claudia hoped I would eventually come to love her."

"And would you?"

"I will never know now, will I?"

"We must get you out of here," Joanna declared.

Tony gave her a bleak smile. "The magistrates' hearing is in a few days' time. I can stand it until then. Indeed, it feels like fit punishment," he added.

"For what?"

"For letting Ned down . . . for wasting what little money I had. For not loving Claudia. I feel that most strongly of all. That somehow I am responsible for her death. That had she not met me, she would still be alive."

"That is nonsense, Tony. She was probably killed by an intruder."

"Oh, I know it makes no logical sense, Jo. But knowing that doesn't change my feelings." Tony stood up. "Now, you must leave before your parents discover what you've been up to. I am sure I will be released at the hearing. After all, there is no real evidence against me."

"But even if they let you go, Tony, you are ruined unless someone finds the real killer."

Tony looked at her, his eyes devoid of emotion. "Yes, I suppose I am. But I find I don't care. All that I care about is gone . . . Ned, Claudia . . . Ashford. I intend to go home and continue the fight for Ashford Ned's way. Maybe that will make up for some of this."

Joanna looked stricken. "And what of our friendship, Tony? Does that count for nothing?"

"My dearest Jo, it is so much a part of my life that I assumed you would take the importance for granted," he said softly.

"No one likes to be taken for granted, Tony."

"You are quite right. I would offer you my hand, Jo, but I am filthy and my clothes smell and I don't want to come close. But I am so very grateful to you for coming. Your visit will get me through the next few days."

Tony opened the door and summoned the gatesman. "I will wait here. Please go with Lady Joanna and summon her a cab home. Here." Tony reached into his pocket and pulled out enough money to pay both the turnkey and the cabdriver. Joanna protested, but he insisted. "It is the least I can do, Jo, to repay your generosity."

But when Joanna was asked her destination by the cabdriver, instead of giving him her address, she directed him to Bow Street. And when her abigail gasped, she only said, "Hush, Sally, and I'll give you an extra allowance this month."

17

When they arrived at the Bow Street Court, Joanna went straight to the magistrate's clerk, who looked shocked to see a lady in the building.

"I understand it is possible for a private citizen to hire a Runner?"

"Yes, my lady."

"Well, that is what I wish to do, then. What is the usual fee?"

"A guinea a week, my lady, plus expenses."

"And do you have any recommendations?"

The clerk looked nonplussed for a moment. "Uh, what sort of investigation are you talking about, ma'am?"

"Murder," Joanna replied bluntly.

The clerk's eyes opened wide. He had not thought it more than a case of a philandering husband. Although, come to think about it, the lady wore no wedding ring.

"Murder, is it? Well, then McManus or Naylor is your man. Except McManus is in Kent, so ... "

"Naylor it is?" said Joanna with a touch of dry humor in her voice. "And where would I find Mr. Naylor?"

"At this time of day, he is usually at the Garrick's Head having a pint."

Joanna's face fell. It was one thing to come to Bow Street. It was quite another to enter a public house. And she could hardly send Sally. She should have brought a footman with her instead.

The clerk saw her consternation. "Don't you worry, my

lady. I can send someone over for you. Let me show you into a quiet room, and I will send Naylor in to you."

Joanna gave him a grateful smile, and pulling at the long-suffering Sally, followed the clerk down the hall.

"Well, this is better than the visitors' quarters at Newgate," she said with a laugh.

"Never tell me you were there, my lady," the clerk said, horrified.

"We just came from there. And my errand is urgent."

"Yes, yes. I will send Jake over right away. Just you wait here."

"Your parents would die, my lady, did they know you was here," said Sally, finally driven to protest.

"But they won't know, Sally," Joanna said patiently. "Not unless you tell them."

"Of course I won't, my lady, not even if you were to take away my afternoon off. I am just trying to say that this is not a place for a lady to be," Sally replied, indignant that her mistress would doubt her loyalty.

They waited a few minutes and then there was a soft knock at the door.

"Come in," said Joanna.

A slight, average-height, rather nondescript man entered the room.

"Lady Joanna Barrand?"

"You must be Jake. I take it you could not find Mr. Naylor? Perhaps I could leave a note asking him to call on me?"

The man grinned. "I am Gideon Naylor, my lady."

"You can't be," Joanna protested without thinking.

"But I am. I understand you wish to hire me for an investigation?"

"Yes, but it is a murder investigation. Perhaps I should wait until Mr. McManus is back from the country." Joanna realized what she had said. "I apologize if I sound insulting, Mr. Naylor, but I need someone . . ."

"Large and threatening?" he asked humorously.

"I had expected a Runner to be more distinctive," she admitted. "Of course, the clerk did recommend you also."

"Yes, well, it has been said of me as well as McManus that I can be 'mild with the mild and terrible with the terrible,' Lady Joanna. But if you wish to wait a few days . . ."

"Oh, dear, I have been very rude, I know, but I do not have the time to wait, so I suppose you will do." Joanna laughed. "That was not much better, was it, Mr. Naylor. I am sorry, but I am quite distraught over the situation of a dear friend. Please sit down."

Naylor sat. There was a sharp knock on the door, and the Runner said: "I have taken the liberty to ask Jake to bring us some tea. I hope that is all right?"

"Why, yes, thank you." Joanna was grateful for his thoughtfulness, and realized that a stimulant was just what she needed.

The door opened and a hulking brute of a man set down a tray. He looked as if he could lift Naylor up with one hand as easily as he carried the tray, but his manner was very respectful.

After he left, Naylor looked over at Joanna and lifted his eyebrows inquiringly.

She laughed. "Yes. All right. That is what I thought a Runner would look like."

"Jake is a very useful man to have around a courtroom," said Naylor, as he poured the tea. "And is often helpful in subduing the occasional suspect. But he has no talent for investigation, my lady. And I assume that is what you want."

Joanna took a sip of her tea. It was surprisingly good and the warmth and strength of it relaxed her. It had been a horrible afternoon. She had never seen Newgate before, much less visited. Nor had she ever imagined she would be sitting in a questioning room drinking tea with a Bow Street Runner. Good tea at that, she thought to herself with a smile.

There was a quiet air of competence about Mr. Naylor, she had to admit. As the tea relaxed some of her tension, sitting with him was beginning to do the same. He seemed willing to sit there, sipping tea, waiting all afternoon, if need be, to hear her story.

"I need someone to investigate a murder of which an old friend has been unjustly accused," she finally stated.

"And what murder would that be, my lady?" Naylor was sure he knew, for he didn't think Lady Joanna Barrand was here on behalf of some lower-class criminal accused of murdering a prostitute, for instance. The only recent murder he knew she might be concerned with was the one for which he'd arrested Lord Ashford.

"The victim was Lady Fairhaven, Mr. Naylor."

"And Lord Ashford is a friend of yours?"

"Then you know of the case," Joanna said eagerly.

"You might say so. I was the one who arrested Lord Ashford."

Joanna was taken aback. "How can I hire you then if you are convinced of Tony's guilt."

"I was the Runner assigned, Lady Joanna. My responsibilities were to investigate and make an arrest on the basis of available evidence. There was enough to incriminate Lord Ashford. That does not mean I am entirely convinced of his guilt. Only that I had to do my duty."

"Then you don't believe he did it?"

"I didn't say that. But I do agree that the case warrants some investigation. Even if—especially if—he is acquitted at the hearing."

"Is there any chance he might be?" Joanna asked.

"It is possible. It was certainly reasonable to arrest him. But to bind a peer over for trial? That might take something like an eyewitness, which we don't have in this case."

"What exactly do you have?"

"As far as we know, Lord Ashford was the last person to see Lady Fairhaven alive. We also know that she had refused him money which he desperately needed. And given his experience as a soldier, he had the expertise to kill her the way someone did."

"I thought she was strangled. Surely anyone could have done that."

Naylor leaned over and placed his hands on Joanna's neck. His thumbs rested on both sides of her throat and she could feel her pulse quicken as he pressed gently. "There are arteries on each side of the neck, my lady. A little pressure from me, and you would lose consciousness. A little more, and you would never regain it. And a soldier is more likely to know this."

Naylor was very gentle in his little demonstration, but Joanna could feel the strength behind his hands. All of a sudden, she realized that it was true: this small, mild man was quite capable of being terrible with the terrible.

She swallowed nervously and he dropped his hands.

"You yourself seem quite expert, Mr. Naylor," she said, her outward calm not betraying how shaken she was. What must it have been like for Claudia in those last few seconds of life?

"I was with the Forty-seventh Foot, my lady. So, yes, I have had some experience. As has Lord Ashford."

"It does sound damning, hearing you recite the evidence. But I know Tony Varden. I know he cared about Lady Fairhaven. I know he could never have killed her, no matter how desperate he was."

"Gamblers can be driven to crime just like drunkards, Lady Joanna. I have seen it before. In a moment of panic, who knows what Lord Ashford might have done?"

"But if he *didn't* do it, then the real murderer is getting away! Tony says he and Claudia came to an understanding. That she gave him the money freely. That . . . " Joanna hesitated, because it was so painful. "That when he left, they were betrothed."

"Yes."

"And you don't believe him?"

"He was quite convincing, Lady Joanna. But you see, there are no witnesses to the reconciliation, only to the quarrel. Of course," Naylor went on, almost to himself, "that in itself is interesting."

"Why?"

"Because the footman would have been able to tell us if Lord Ashford left looking like a newly betrothed man. If Lady Fairhaven appeared happy or angry or disappointed. But he has disappeared."

"What do you mean," demanded Joanna.

"Lady Fairhaven had hired a new under-footman only a few weeks ago. The butler instructed him to remain at the door, and see Lady Fairhaven up to her room. But when I got there, I found that this Jim had vanished, taking nothing with him. Apparently he had not even gone up to his room that night."

"Then maybe *he* did it," said Joanna, hope rising in her voice.

"But why?"

"For the money, of course."

"Perhaps. Although we don't know how much money Lady Fairhaven had in the drawer. And Jim may be lying dead in a gutter somewhere for all we know. At any rate, the motive for him is less clear."

"Isn't there anyone else?"

"An intruder. There has been a rash of burglaries in the last few months. But the men I know who work that neighborhood are not usually violent." Naylor hesitated. "There is the new Lord Fairhaven . . . "

Joanna shuddered.

"You don't like the earl, I take it?" commented Naylor with a smile.

"No, there is something very cold about him. I could well imagine him as the murderer," said Joanna.

"Unfortunately, Lady Joanna, your dislike of Lord Fairhaven's temperament is not evidence. However, a little investigation into the background of the late Lord Fairhaven's will might be in order. And a search for this missing footman. If you still wish to hire me, I will take on the case."

Joanna's face lit up. "Thank you, Mr. Naylor. I cannot tell you how much this means to me. Even if Tony is released, he will be tainted by suspicion and hounded by the gossips unless the true murderer is found. He is an old and dear friend," she said softly. "He suffered enough from his father and brother's deaths. You will begin immediately, I hope," she added, standing up and summoning Sally.

"Yes. Lord Ashford is fortunate to have such a devoted friend, Lady Joanna," said Naylor, as he showed the women out. *And if I were a gambler myself,* he thought, as he handed Joanna into a cab, *I would bet that Lord Ashford has much more than your friendship, my lady.*

Luckily, when Joanna returned home, her father was at his club and her mother was taking an afternoon nap. At some point she would probably have to tell them about her visits, but today she was not up to it. As soon as she reached her room, Sally helped her out of her gown.

"Burn it, Sally," said Joanna, as she stepped out of it. "I may be imagining things, but to me, it smells like Newgate."

"Yes, my lady."

"And Sally," Joanna added.

"Yes, my lady?"

"Thank you for accompanying me. I know it was distressing for you, but I couldn't have done it alone. I appreciate your loyalty."

Sally flushed with pleasure. "I am just glad that we are both home safe and sound," she replied.

Joanna dismissed her, and pulling on her silk wrapper, sat down in the chair by her window. Her room overlooked the small garden in back of the house, and she liked to read by the window, or just sit, taking in the peace and beauty of the knot garden and the roses. Today, however, she was blind to the colors, and the only smell she was conscious of, despite the open window, was the remembered stench of the prison.

The energy that had carried her through the afternoon was gone. She was exhausted. And heartsick. For years she had been hoping that Tony might one day *see* her as the woman she had become. The woman who had been in love with him since childhood. She smiled as she saw herself so many years ago kicking his shins and pounding him with her fists. That was the only time she had showed him a passionate response. When she had been dreaming of Tony as her devoted Lancelot, imaging what it would be like to be lifted up in front of him and ride away. She never did get beyond being held tenderly as he guided his horse homeward. And then, there he was, apologizing and laughing at the same time, no "parfit, gentil knight" at all, and that was when she knew she loved him. Oh, she would have been better off going after Ned, who at least was genuinely apologetic. But Ned was too stable, too good. Tony was volatile and funny and attractive.

It had always been hopeless, and Joanna had thought she had resigned herself to her small place in Tony's heart. Even watching his pursuit of Lady Fairhaven, she had almost convinced herself that it was only for the money. But today her defenses were down. He had cared about Claudia. Maybe not loved her, but cared about her, he said, as he cared about Joanna. But it was Claudia to whom he had become betrothed. Only for a few short hours, but had it not been for an intruder, Tony would have married her. Because she had enough money to save Ashford, and Joanna did not.

It seemed to Joanna that figuratively she was still tied to that damned tree, waiting and waiting for Tony to remember her. To realize that he had left someone of importance to him behind. But he was still a careless and stupid, stupid man, thought Joanna, wishing she had him in front of her right now. She wanted to rail at him, kick his shins again, and this time tell him: "Here I am, and I love you, you fool!"

But now he was a prisoner. Now he was waiting too.

Love was too hard, she thought, as her anger subsided and as the tears began. They ran down her face slowly and then more rapidly, and she watched from someplace far away as they fell on the green silk, puckering the material.

It was too hard to keep it all hidden. To maintain her cool facade. To pretend that all she felt for him was what he felt for her.

She could walk away, of course. Hope that Naylor's investigation paid off, but when Tony was released, cut him the way most of society would. No, she could never do that. But she could go away. She had been promising a visit to her godmother in Cumbria for a long time. She would see to Tony's release and then, once the Season was over, get away from him for the summer. And come home free of her ridiculous, childish obsession at last.

18

Mark Halesworth was furious. He had visited Reresby, Justin's solicitor, the day after Claudia's death to inquire about her will. He was hoping that she had not gotten around to making one, which would make his inheritance automatic. But Reresby would never have let her get away with such carelessness, of course. He was too efficient, damn him. "Lady Fairhaven made out a will immediately after the late earl's death, my lord," the solicitor had informed him.

"I see." Mark breathed a sigh of relief. It would take longer to see the money, but Claudia could have left her money to no one but him.

"Of course, she made a few changes a few weeks before she died," added Reresby. The old man heartily disliked the present Lord Fairhaven, and took great satisfaction in giving him the bad news.

"A few changes? What kind of changes?"

"Oh, I am afraid I am not at liberty to say, sir. There won't be an official reading of the will until the mystery of her death is resolved."

"Mystery? What mystery? She was murdered, you fool. They have arrested Tony Varden for the crime."

"Only on suspicion, my lord. He has not yet been bound over for trial."

"I am sure he will be."

"That may be so, but in a case such as this, the will must wait."

"Then you will not show it to me?"

"No, my lord."

Mark turned on his heel and slammed the door behind him. Old Reresby smiled a dry little smile as he pulled open his drawer and fingered the vellum document within. Lord Fairhaven might be angry now, but he would be far angrier when he heard the changes Lady Fairhaven had made. It was anyone's guess, of course, what Tony Varden would feel. Even if he was released, the will could be reason enough to put him right back in jail.

"I wish to see Mr. Gideon Naylor."

The magistrate's clerk looked up in surprise. Within two days, Naylor had had two visitors. That's what happened when one of the nobility was killed, he thought.

"Mr. Naylor is out on a case, Mr. . . . . ?"

"Mark Halesworth, Lord Fairhaven. If I leave him a note, will you see that he gets it?"

"Of course, my lord."

The clerk handed Mark a piece of paper and a pen with a worn-down nib which spattered while Mark wrote.

"There," he said, frowning at his ink-stained fingers. "See that he gets this as soon as possible."

"Yes, my lord."

The clerk waited until Fairhaven had been gone a full five minutes before unfolding the note.

Naylor,
 I suggest you visit Reresby, my cousin's solicitors. Lady Fairhaven made some changes in her will which might have given Lord Ashford even more of a reason to kill her.
   Fairhaven

Hmmm, thought the clerk, *Gideon is being pushed from both sides. I wonder how he will fall.*

A day later, Gideon himself was wondering too. He had returned to Lady Fairhaven's house and obtained all the information he could about Jim, which was, unfortunately, minimal. The previous under-footman had left suddenly and recommended James Tolin. "He was a bright lad, and very eager to please," said Dawson. "And he quickly developed the same loyalty to the mistress as we all had," the butler added, with a cough to distract from the slight tremor of emotion in his voice.

"Did he come from London, do you know? Did he ever mention family?"

"I know he visited family on his day off," replied Dawson. "But he never told us where in the city they lived. He did say something once about his father also having been in service."

"Thank you, Dawson, that gives me a little something to go on. Now, would he have had any money to get him by?"

"Whatever was left of his wages."

"Which we found hidden away in his room," Naylor reminded the butler.

Dawson frowned. "What if Jim saw Lord Ashford killing the mistress and Lord Ashford bribed him to disappear and stay quiet? Have you thought of that possibility, Mr. Naylor?" he asked.

"So maybe he wasn't as loyal as you thought?"

"Well, he was new, and almost anyone can be bought."

"It is a possibility to be considered, Mr. Dawson," said Naylor, with a grateful smile. He always enjoyed watching people begin to enter into an investigation, each sure that he or she had thought of the solution. "In the meantime," he said, "if you hear anything or think of anything else, be sure to be in touch with me."

"Of course, Mr. Naylor."

Naylor paused on the stoop. He would start inquiring after older footmen named Tolin. If he were lucky, Jim's father would have been employed in Mayfair and not by some rich Cit. This part of the job, the tramping about and collecting information, was the most necessary and also the most tedious. But at least it kept him fit and trim, he thought.

After a day and a half of interviewing dozens of households and coming up with nothing, however, he decided to give himself a break and follow up on Lord Fairhaven's lead.

Of course, the old solicitor would not show Gideon the will, but he confirmed the fact that Lady Fairhaven had made recent changes, which in itself was significant.

"Can you tell me if and how much Lord Ashford would benefit under this new will, Mr. Reresby?"

"I am not free to tell you *how much* Lord Ashford would benefit," responded the solicitor.

"I will have to wait for the reading, then. Thank you, Mr. Reresby. You have been most helpful."

"I hope so, Mr. Naylor."

So she changed her will to benefit Ashford, thought Gideon. *I am afraid, Lady Joanna, things are not looking good for your old friend. If he knew about the will . . .*

Gideon hailed a cab and directed the driver to Newgate.

19

Tony, who had been trying to ignore the cries of a new prisoner who sounded as if he belonged in Bedlam, not Newgate, was struggling to get through the meditations of Marcus Aurelius. Joanna had sent over several books, and he still couldn't figure out whether they represented her attempts at humor or whether she seriously thought he might find them valuable. At any rate, the old Roman was better than Foxe's *Martyrs* and William Law's *Call to a Devout and Holy Life*—but just barely. Tony supposed that *in extremis* a man should be turning to God or philosophy, but he himself thought a laugh would have done him a lot more good. His situation was serious enough, thank you. He was about ready to pitch the book and look for a game of cards, which he had sworn to avoid, when he was summoned to the visitors' room.

His face fell when he saw that it was not Joanna but the Bow Street Runner who had brought him here.

"What do you want, Naylor?" he asked with barely veiled hostility.

"I want to ask you a few more questions, my lord," Gideon answered in neutral tones. "Lady Joanna Barrand has employed me on your behalf."

Tony felt more humiliated than when he had been arrested, if that were possible. Here he was, helpless, and Joanna was likely paying Naylor out of her allowance. He didn't think he could stand to be so beholden to her, and instead of feeling grateful, he felt angry.

"I will not have it," he declared. "Consider yourself dismissed."

Naylor looked up at Tony with his mild blue eyes. "Please sit down, my lord. I am afraid," he added with a quick smile, "that it is not in your power to dismiss me, since you are not the one who has hired me."

"How could Joanna do this?" asked Tony as he seated himself on the chair.

"I rather think she did this to help you," said Naylor ironically. "Is there something you don't wish me to be investigating, my lord?" he added mildly, which caused Tony to look at him more closely.

"You are a deceptively mild man, aren't you, Naylor?"

"It has been remarked upon before," admitted Gideon. "Now, my lord, if you are innocent, it can only benefit you if I investigate further."

"I just can't bear being beholden to Joanna," groaned Tony.

"Taking money from Lady Fairhaven didn't seem to bother you."

"Damn you, Naylor. She *loved* me. I knew that I had something to give her in return. My friendship and affection were hers."

"And you have no affection for Lady Joanna? I thought you have been friends since childhood."

"Of course I care about her, but it is an entirely different situation. She is an unmarried young lady whose reputation would be ruined should this get out. And she doesn't love me in the same way Claudia did."

Gideon wanted to shake Ashford. What a fool the man was. Within minutes of sitting with the lady, it had been obvious to Gideon that she was in love with the young idiot. And after years of friendship, the man was still oblivious!

"Look, Naylor," Tony continued. "I know I don't sound very admirable. I sound like an arrogant fortune hunter, in fact. But it wasn't like that. Lady Fairhaven and I were good friends. There was love on her side and affection on mine, which we both hoped would develop into something stronger after we married. She knew I needed her money to save Ashford, but she also knew that I cared about her. She could have done far worse, after all."

"Like Lord Fairhaven?"

"He was not her choice. Her parents sold her when she was only seventeen, although it turned out to be a very happy marriage, from what she told me."

"No, I meant the present Lord Fairhaven."

"Mark Halesworth!"

"You don't like him?"

"That is putting it as mild as you appear, Naylor," said Tony with a grin. "I knew him in school. He is a cold fish and interested only in money."

"Now tell me again what happened that night," Gideon asked, dropping the topic of Lord Fairhaven for the moment.

"I've already told you all."

"Tell me again."

Tony sighed. It was painful to go over it again. "I had borrowed money from Claudia earlier that week. And promised to pay off my debts. I didn't. I went back to the tables and lost it all and then won back a part of it. I had to face her with that, which wasn't easy." Tony hesitated.

"Go on."

"I was just thinking that if I hadn't broken my promise, she might still be alive. But then, how could an outside intruder have known about the money?"

"Indeed."

"I don't know why we are going over this again, since you clearly believe I am guilty, Naylor. Joanna is wasting her money."

"Continue, my lord," said Gideon, softly but firmly.

"I called on Claudia the next night to ask her for more money. We went into the library. Dawson came in with brandy right in the middle of an argument. He would have heard her refuse me the money. That is certainly true. But then she sent him off to bed. We talked for a while and I convinced her that *this* time I really did mean to give up gaming. That I would pay off my immediate debts and stay out of the hells. And we became betrothed." Tony stopped.

"And . . ."

"I can't really believe it, you know," he said with tears in his eyes. "That she is dead. There is a part of me that thinks this is a very long and particularly bad nightmare and that when I wake up, Claudia will be there."

"What happened then?" Naylor was insistent.

Tony passed a hand over his eyes. "I said good night, and I left. Jim let me out."

"The new footman?"

"Yes."

"Did you give him any money, my lord?"

"I slipped him a guinea, I was so happy about the betrothal."

"And then you left?"

"And then I left."

"Supposing that this were true . . ."

"It is, damn it, it *is*!"

"Then who do you think killed her?"

"I don't know. There have been a number of housebreakings in the neighborhood recently. Couldn't it have been a thief, not expecting anyone to be awake?"

"And what of Jim? He has completely disappeared."

Tony frowned. "I would not have thought him the sort to be capable of murder. He seemed to care about Claudia, as did all of her servants."

"And Lord Fairhaven?" asked Gideon, keeping his voice even and uninflected.

"I would like to say, of course, it was Mark. I *don't* like him. But what would be his motive?"

"Money. The commonest of motives, I am afraid," said Gideon with a rueful smile. "Lady Fairhaven inherited a fortune when her husband died."

"Yes, but Mark is quite wealthy in his own right. He inherited the estate, the title, and takes in quite a bit from the business. What more could he want?"

"For some people, when it comes to wealth, there is never enough," commented Gideon. "What of Lady Fairhaven's will?"

Tony looked blankly at him, and Gideon thought to himself that either he was a very good actor, Lord Ashford, or he was telling the truth. And he gave equal weight to each possibility at the moment.

"Would she even have made out a will yet? After all, she was a relatively young widow."

"But a very wealthy one. The Fairhaven solicitor saw to that. Mark Halesworth was to inherit everything in the case of her death, should she not remarry and have children."

"So he stands to inherit all now? Doesn't that give him a strong motive?" asked Tony.

"It might. Except that evidently Lady Fairhaven made some changes in her will in the last two weeks. I do not know the details, but I understand they were to your benefit, my lord."

Tony's eyes widened. "But we weren't even betrothed at that point."

"You seem to be telling the truth about one thing, my lord. Lady Fairhaven did indeed love you. My guess is that she left you enough, whatever happened between you, to save your estate. It is unfortunate, however, that she could not foresee her murder . . ."

"Well, I am a dead man then," said Tony, getting up from the table.

"Not yet. The will has not yet been read. If it is not read before the hearing, you may well be freed."

"And then arrested again immediately after!"

"Not if I can find any evidence that points to someone else, my lord."

"It is hopeless, Naylor."

Naylor sighed. "You have so little faith in my abilities, my lord."

Tony had to laugh at the patently mocking tone in Naylor's voice.

"I admit your situation is not good. But neither is it hopeless."

"Do me a favor, Naylor."

"Yes, my lord."

"You will no doubt be reporting back to Lady Joanna?"

"Yes, my lord."

"Ask her to send me Miss Austen's latest, will you? I don't think I can go back to Marcus Aurelius after this."

20

Joanna smiled when Naylor conveyed Tony's request.

"Tony is not drawn to the stoic Roman? Well, I suppose I am not surprised. Marcus Aurelius was one of Ned's favorites. Tony preferred Caesar and his battles. How did you find him otherwise, Mr. Naylor?" Joanna asked, motioning the Runner to sit down.

"He has little enough confidence in my skills, my lady. Or else he knows there is no one else out there to find."

"And which do you think is the truth?"

"I try to stay open-minded, my lady, while I am investigating a case. There was certainly enough evidence against Lord Ashford to arrest him. Whether there is enough to hold him is for the judges to decide."

"But having talked to Tony again, you cannot possibly believe that he is a murderer," protested Joanna.

Gideon looked very different for a moment or two, his face hard, his eyes sharp. "I have proved the most innocent-seeming men and women guilty of horrendous crimes, my lady."

Joanna shivered. It seemed that Naylor was seeing, right then in his imagination, deeds bloody and violent. Then his face softened. "But I must admit that Lord Ashford is most convincing in his protestations of innocence."

Joanna breathed a deep sigh of relief. "Have you discovered anything about the missing footman?"

"Not yet. In fact, that is what I will be concentrating on again tomorrow."

"Thank you, Mr. Naylor, for all your efforts," said Joanna, summoning the butler to show Naylor out.

She sat there in the library for a while. The hearing was in a few days. How on earth could Naylor find out anything by then? What if this Jim were dead or had fled London? What if he hadn't seen anything at all? Then Tony might be bound over for trial, and quite possibly hanged. And she would have to live out the remainder of her life without him.

Gideon started early the next morning. About to break for a pint and a steak-and-kidney pie, he tried one more house on Curzon Street. At first, it seemed as if in all the households: no one could remember an older footman named Tolin. But then the cook, who had been working there for years, said, "Wait a minute, Mr. Naylor. Does it have to be a footman?"

"What do you mean?" Gideon asked.

"Years ago I knew a house parlormaid by that name. She would be about the right age now to be this lad Jim's mother."

Gideon's face brightened. "Used his mother's name perhaps? That in itself is very interesting. Do you remember what happened to her?"

"She married the footman from the Pentlow household. But I don't remember what happened to her after that."

"And what was the footman's name?"

By this time all of the servants were holding their breath. Imagine old Mrs. Conklin being able to help solve a murder case.

"Crook? No. But something like that. Let me think . . ."

Gideon waited patiently as Mrs. Conklin screwed up her face and closed her eyes.

"Rooke. That were it. Henry Rooke. He was a very handsome young footman. I don't blame her for running off with him."

The butler pounded Mrs. Conklin on the back. "Good for

you, Mrs. Conklin. You just might have solved the case, eh, Mr. Naylor?"

Gideon grinned. "Not yet. But this may make it a lot easier."

And it did. He only had to retrace his steps and give the correct name at a few houses before he came to one where an older servant remembered the Rookes very well.

"He worked for Sir Horace Pentlow for many years, sir. But he retired a few years ago."

Gideon was off. Sir Horace lived only a few streets away, and by this time he was too intent on finding Jim's parents to pay attention to his protesting stomach.

Sir Horace was at home, and when he was reassured that no information he gave would be used against his old servants, he gave Gideon their address.

The Rookes lived in the first small house next to a pub off the King's Road. The Bird and Whistle. Gideon could smell the ale and decided, since it was now almost suppertime, he could justify a short detour. The Rookes would likely be home having their own tea or supper anyway.

He took a window seat and watched the residents of the street come and go. It was a poor neighborhood, but respectable, and he felt much more at home in this pub than he had in Lady Joanna's library, although she would never have guessed it. That was one thing about being a Runner, thought Gideon. You dealt with such riffraff all day that a street like this felt like a corner of Mayfair. And what was he, after all, but an old west-country man? His own father had been in service to the local squire: his head groom. Gideon could have stayed and worked his way up, either in the stables or the house, but couldn't stand the idea of not being his own master. When the recruiters came by one day, he just up and left. Of course, he had hardly considered the fact that in the army one was not one's own master! And the irony was, with all his knowledge of horses, he ended up on the 47th Foot. He had seen a bit of the world, both beautiful and awful, and when he returned to Somerset, he found his mother dead and his father pensioned off.

There was nothing for him at home, and so after a long visit during which he stayed with his sister (she had married a neighboring farmer) and enjoyed being Uncle Gideon to her children, he took off for London. He had heard of the Runners and knew that an ex-soldier had a good chance of being hired. He could have applied for the horse patrol, but liked the greater freedom the Runners had, traveling all over England. So here he was still, with aching and swollen feet, he thought, as he wiggled his toes in his boots.

He wondered if Jim would have taken refuge with his parents. Well, he would soon find out, he thought, as he rose and left his money beside his plate.

A few minutes later he was knocking on their door. They were on the second floor, just above a small butcher shop. Mr. Rooke, who answered the door, might well have been a footman still, with his straight posture and expressionless face. His eyebrows lifted, however, when he recognized Gideon as a Robin Redbreast.

"Mr. Henry Rooke?"

The old man nodded.

"I am Gideon Naylor of Bow Street. I need to ask you a few questions. May I come in?"

Mr. Rooke pulled the door open and Gideon followed him into the parlor.

"How can I help you, Mr. Naylor?" asked the old man, sounding puzzled.

"You have a son, Jim, I believe?"

The mask dropped, and a concerned father, not a well-trained servant, stood in front of Gideon.

"Nothing has happened to our Jim, has it?" he asked, his voice lowered.

"I have no reason to believe so. Yet," added Gideon, "it is just that he has disappeared from his place of employment rather suddenly. And I need to ask him some questions."

"From Halesworth's?"

"Yes, three nights ago. The butler left him in charge when he retired for the evening, and Jim was gone in the morning. He had never even gone up to his room, according to the other footman. He could still be in his livery, as a matter of fact," said Gideon slowly, not having thought of that. Although, he immediately said to himself, if he were indeed still in his livery, he might well be dead.

"What do you mean, the other footman? Livery? You must have the wrong Jim, Mr. Naylor. My son is not in the service."

"But *you* mentioned the Halesworths," said Gideon.

"Yes. Halesworth Limited Jim is a clerk there," said his father proudly. "We sent him to school so he would not have to follow us into service."

"Your son, Jim Rooke, works as a clerk in Mark Halesworth's—Lord Fairhaven's—firm?"

"Yes, sir. Has done for some months."

"When did you last see Jim?"

The older man frowned. "He usually comes home every Sunday, but these last few weeks he has been coming over on Wednesday afternoons."

"And he never told you he was working in Lady Fairhaven's household as an under-footman?"

"No!"

"Well, he was. And on the night of the murder, he was the last one to see her alive, except for the murderer and Lord Ashford. Unless Lord Ashford *is* her murderer," added Naylor under his breath. "Thank you, Mr. Rooke, you have been a great help to me."

"Wait, wait, Mr. Naylor. You mean to tell me our Jim is mixed up in a Mayfair murder and you don't know where he is?"

"Not yet, but I intend to find out."

21

When Jim had run from the house on the night of the murder, he had, in fact, thought of taking refuge with his parents. Then he realized how obvious a place it would be to hide. If he went there, he would likely be found immediately, by the Runners or by Lord Fairhaven. Of the two, he preferred the Runners, he thought, as he remembered the scene in the library.

He was very lucky Lord Ashford was a generous man, for here he was, a fugitive from justice, with no clothes on his back but the Fairhaven livery, which would make him memorable to anyone who saw him.

He had turned down a deserted alley halfway between his parents' house and the Fairhaven town house and decided it was as good a place as any to spend what was left of the night. He huddled against a building and tried to ignore the sounds of the rats and the smell of the sewer. When the sun rose, he took off his jacket and was about to leave it in the alley when he realized he could probably get good money for it in Petticoat Lane. So he put it over an arm and made his way to the market.

The old-clothesmen were shrewd bargainers and Jim ended up making an even trade, rather than getting a few shillings extra for what was obviously the better suit of clothes, livery or not. But at least he hadn't had to spend anything. And thank goodness, he'd remembered the half-crown in his breeches pocket from Lord Fairhaven, before he handed over the clothes.

At the thought of Fairhaven, Jim could almost feel his

heart start and stop again. Lady Claudia Fairhaven was dead, and she had been such a lovely woman and very kind to him as a new footman. Why had he ever agreed to spy on her in the first place?

Of course, Lord Fairhaven had convinced him that it was for her own good, that she was being taken advantage of by Lord Ashford. But from what Jim had seen, Lord Ashford had been very fond of his mistress and she, most certainly, had been enamored of him. And Lord Ashford had been very happy that night when he left, giving Jim a generous vail and saying: "I finally have something to celebrate, Jim, so you should too." He had leaned forward and whispered: "I've proposed and she's accepted and you may be the first to wish me happy. But mum's the word." He'd smiled and winked and Jim had grinned back. Lord Fairhaven would not be happy with the news, but Jim couldn't but feel that it was a good thing for Lady Fairhaven to have such a handsome and charming man in her house. And her bed.

He hadn't even had time to inform Lord Fairhaven, who had arrived shortly thereafter and gone right to the library, saying that there was no need to announce him. And then, that awful sight of his mistress being laid on the floor. Thank God Fairhaven had been too involved to notice the door quietly opening and closing.

Perhaps it was foolish to have run, but how could he have gone back to his post, handed Lord Fairhaven his coat, and pretended nothing was wrong? And what if he had been seen? Any man who would kill a woman would have no compunction about getting rid of a young, naive, and stupid clerk.

For he had been stupid. Stupid to believe his employer.

But no matter now, thought Jim. Done was done. He had to find a place to hide while he thought of what to do.

He had heard of St. Giles. Certainly if he went there, he'd be just one more criminal and hard to find. But he wasn't a real criminal, he protested to himself. And, to tell the truth, he was too scared to walk the worst streets of the city. Perhaps on the edges of St. Giles he could find something. A cheap boarding house where he could rent a room.

He ended up south of Russell Square. He walked down several streets and then stopped in a corner pub for a glass of ale. He hadn't eaten since last night's supper, and the ale went right to his head. He had intended to save his money and eat only once a day, but decided to make an exception and ordered a plate of bread and cheese. When the barmaid brought him his food, he smiled at her and said he was new to the neighborhood and looking for a place to say. Did she know of anyone who'd be willing to rent him a room?

"There's Mrs. Jarvison's. Or Mrs. Spencer's," she said with a mischievous glint in her eye. "Mrs. Spencer always has rooms, although you may have to share," she added with a wink.

"Oh, I don't mind sharing," said Jim, thinking what a good-natured girl she was. "Bucknall Street, you said?"

"Yes, sir."

The food and drink had revived him, but Jim wanted to find a place quickly so he'd be off the streets. He decided to go straight to this Mrs. Spencer's, since it was closer.

Number 17 Bucknall Street was a small house which stood out from the others on the street because of its newly whitewashed bricks and the cleanliness of its windows. Jim knocked at the door, which was opened by a young woman who appeared somewhat overdressed for a maid. Overdressed and underdressed, thought Jim, trying not to look at what the girl's low bodice revealed.

"Can I help you sir?" she asked.

"I am looking for a Mrs. Spencer," Jim responded. "I understand she has rooms available."

The girl laughed. "You might put it that way. Come in, sir, and I'll get Mrs. Spencer."

Jim was shown into the parlor, a very tastefully decorated room. The place seemed clean and respectable, and with a very pretty print on the wall, Jim thought as he gazed at the light-filled landscape.

"That is a Constable," said a clear, strong voice behind him.

At the word, "constable" Jim almost jumped out of his new and rather ill-fitting suit.

"Constable? Where?" he asked without thinking, as he turned and faced Mrs. Spencer, or so he assumed her to be. How could anyone have found him so quickly? He glanced around the room. There was no place to hide. He was about ready to push past her when she said, more gently:

"John Constable, the painter. You seemed to be admiring my painting, Mr. . . . ?

"Oh, yes, uh, of course," Jim stammered. "Jim . . . Jones, ma'am."

Mrs. Spencer smiled. "Mr. . . . Jones, then. I understand you are looking for a . . . room."

"Yes. How much do you charge per night?"

"It depends on what you want, Mr. Jones."

"Nothing fancy. And breakfast in the morning?"

"You sound easy enough to satisfy, Mr. Jones. This is perhaps your first time in a house like mine?" Mrs. Spencer inquired.

"Uh, yes. I have never stayed at a boarding house before."

"Well, I have just the . . . room for you, then. Number three, right at the top of the stairs. Ten shillings for the night."

Jim let his breath out. He had been afraid he wouldn't be able to afford such a clean place. "Good, I will take it."

"Carrie will show you up. Enjoy your time with us, Mr. Jones."

Mrs. Spencer opened the parlor door and summoned the buxom young woman who had met Jim at the door.

"Here you are, then," she said, when they reached the top of the first flight of stairs. "A whole night, eh? There's not many who stay more than a few hours. But, then, you are young and perhaps new to the city."

"Er, yes," said Jim, thankful when she left, shutting the door behind her.

He looked around. It was a very nice room. A little overdecorated for his taste, perhaps. A bit odd to have a crimson coverlet and pillow sham, he thought, and the prints on these walls were certainly not landscapes! But it was clean and it was his, and now that his foolish fear had subsided, he felt very safe. He slipped off his shoes and lay back on the bed, which was very comfortable.

There was a soft knock at the door, and without thinking he called, "Come in," expecting the maid with a pitcher of water for the washstand.

Instead, a slight, dark-haired girl entered, dressed even more revealingly than the maid.

"Good evening, Mr. Jones. I am Nancy."

"Good evening, Nancy," said Jim, swinging his legs over the side of the bed and standing up. Could this be Mrs. Spencer's daughter, who acted as some sort of hostess? They had the same dark hair, although this girl's face was freer of cosmetics.

The girl closed the door behind her and drew the latch shut.

"You have the room for the whole night?"

"Yes."

"If you like me, we can spend all of it together," said Nancy, who had put a foot up on the chair in the corner and was beginning to peel off her stockings.

"Together?" Jim wondered if he had drunk more than one tankard of ale without realizing it. And then he remembered the barmaid's wink and her description of Mrs. Spencer's as a place where one sometimes shared a room. He groaned and sat down on the bed. He had taken refuge in a bawdy house!

Nancy came over and sat next to him. "I understand this is your first time, Mr. Jones. Don't worry, I can help you," she reassured him as she started to unbutton his shirt.

Jim shrank back. "No, I mean, I said it was my first time, but I meant in a boarding house, not a bawdy house. There's been a mistake. I must get my money back."

"If you already paid Mrs. Spencer, you won't get it

back," said Nancy matter-of-factly. "But you have the room, whether you want me in it or not," she added with a rueful little smile.

"Oh, it's not that you aren't a pretty girl," protested Jim. "It is just that right now, I don't . . . need one."

"Well, I'd better get Mrs. Spencer and see what we are to do with you." Nancy was gone before Jim could protest.

He groaned again and then laughed. Here he was, a fugitive from both the law and a murderer, locked up in a brothel. And he, raised by two of the most respectable parents one could have.

Of course, he knew such places existed. But he had never even contemplated going to one. No, he had thought that one day he and Polly Hemmings, the daughter of the butcher who owned his parents' flat, might make a match of it. A kiss or two from Polly was all he had experienced with a woman thus far. The image of Nancy's shapely white legs came unbidden to his mind, and he felt a tightening in his groin and was appalled. How could he even think of such a thing? He needed to get his money back and find another room, was what he needed to do. Not sit here and imagine what a pretty young whore would look like with all her clothes off!

The door was opened again, this time by Mrs. Spencer. Her face, which was skillfully made up, looked a little older and harder than it had in the parlor.

"I understand you want your money back, Mr. Jones."

"Yes, you see, there has been a misunderstanding . . ," said Jim, hastily standing up.

"It would seem so. Please sit down." Jim sank back onto the bed and Mrs. Spencer pulled the chair over and sat down also.

"The question is, Mr. Jones, who should pay for the misunderstanding, you or I?"

"Perhaps we could split it?" Jim suggested tentatively. "You see, I don't really have that much money and now I'll have to go and find a real boarding house." he said with a smile.

"You seemed a bit nervous when you arrived, Mr. Jones. And while having no change of clothes is no crime, it seems a bit odd, don't you think? Just what are you running from? I don't want any problems with the law. I run a decent business here and am very careful to keep rough customers away from my girls."

Jim blanched.

"Although you do not look like a hardened criminal to me, Mr. Jones," added Mrs. Spencer with a smile that softened her face and made one focus on her mouth, which was full and tender, in contrast to her businesslike expression. There was an air of sympathy about her, and Jim, without knowing why, decided to confide in her.

"I am not a criminal, Mrs. Spencer . . . or at least, I don't consider myself one. But the law might well be after me."

"For what?"

Jim told his story haltingly.

"You never went back to your parents' house, then?"

"No, I was going to, but then it seemed the first place they would look for me."

"And you used your mother's maiden name at Lady Fairhaven's?"

"Yes."

"Then it may take longer than you think for them to identify you, much less make any connection to Lord Fairhaven. I think you have much more to fear from him than the Runners, Mr. . . . ?"

"Rooke. Yes, I admit I am most afraid of him. Although I am pretty sure he didn't see me."

"No matter if he didn't. You disappear the very night of the murder and you know he was the last person to be admitted into the house. He will wonder why you disappeared."

"Well, it is none of your business," said Jim resolutely. "I will leave right away. And if you could give me half the money back, I would greatly appreciate it."

"I have another proposition for you, Mr. Rooke," said Mrs. Spencer after a moment or two. There was something about the young man that drew her sympathy. "You now have some experience as a footman in a Mayfair household. And a footman answering the door to the gentlemen would add a certain . . . *Je ne sais quoi* to my business, don't you think?" asked Mrs. Spencer with an ironic smile.

As Jim started to splutter a protest, Mrs. Spencer lifted her hand. "You seem to have covered your trail very well. You have a limited amount of money. I can offer you room and board in exchange for a position. My customers are all very respectable, I assure you. If anyone behaves like a ruffian, which is rare, I call my neighbor next door. He is a farrier for the coach company, and large enough to bounce the most troublesome off the premises. And after all, who would ever think to look for you in a bawdy house?"

Jim thought a few minutes and then decided he had no choice. She was right. His money would soon run out and then what would he do? And who would ever track him here?

"My parents would die if they knew. All they ever wanted was for me to be free from a life of service. And here I am gone from clerk to a footman in a brothel in a month!"

Mrs. Spencer laughed, but there was sympathy in her voice when she said: "You are in good company, then, Jim. I may call you Jim? All of us here have suffered rapid changes in circumstance. And Jim, if you will also run errands and help with the shopping, you can have your choice of the girls once a week. Nancy seemed to find you very appealing."

"Er, thank you, Mrs. Spencer, but I think not."

"If you change your mind, let me know . . . And Jim . . ."

"Yes, ma'am?"

"Come downstairs and I'll give you some money for a new suit of clothes. I expect all my employees to be well-dressed, and that suit leaves much to be desired."

22

Tony was roused early on the morning of his hearing. He did his best to clean up and make himself look presentable, but a few days in Newgate, even in a private room, didn't do much for one's appearance. Nor did the handcuffs around his wrists.

He had managed to get the family solicitor to make a brief visit and review the procedures with him. In a magistrates' hearing, unlike a trial, witnesses gave their testimony only before the magistrates, so Tony would not even hear the evidence against him. He sent John off to the War Office to request affidavits and a character witness. Colonel Bain, who had served with Tony in the Peninsula, would at least speak for his loyal service to the Crown and his care for his men.

When they got to Bow Street, he was kept in a separate room for what seemed forever, his hands cuffed, and guarded by an officer of the court.

He could hear doors opening and closing and at one point he thought he heard Gideon Naylor's voice in the corridor. He found himself hoping that Naylor would open the door and pay him a visit. The sight of a familiar face, even if not a particularly friendly one would have been welcome.

It was nerve-racking to sit there and not know what was being said about him, about Claudia. He had never felt so helpless in his life—not even when he and his sergeant had been huddled behind some boulders in the mountains of Spain, hoping that the evening patrol that was walking within a foot of them would pass by.

Finally, after what seemed days, he was summoned before the magistrates. Naylor was there, sitting in the corner, and looking blander than usual. Tony was sworn in and the questioning started.

"Anthony Varden, Lord Ashford?"

"Yes, my lords."

"You understand the charge brought against you?"

"Yes, my lords."

"And what do you answer to this charge?"

"I am not guilty."

Tony at first addressed both magistrates, but only one was asking the questions. The other sat there with his eyes half closed, looking as if he was ready to fall asleep, and Tony was afraid that the questioning was only for form's sake. They had probably decided already to hand him over for trial. And if he was handed over, he would be spending weeks in Newgate.

"Could you please tell this court about your relationship with Lady Fairhaven."

"We were good friends."

"Come, come, Ashford, we want the whole story. When did you meet Lady Fairhaven?"

"We met at the beginning of this Season. She had spent two years in mourning for her husband and had just returned to the city and to a social life. We discovered immediately that we had something in common: we had both lost someone we had loved."

"I presume you mean your brother?"

"Yes, my lord."

"Lady Fairhaven was an older woman, was she not?"

"Only by five years."

"And a rich widow? And you had inherited an impoverished estate?"

Tony nodded.

"Your brother had worked very hard for the recovery of Ashford, had he not?" The magistrate did not wait for an answer. "And what were your methods, once you inherited? Not the same as your brother's, I take it."

"No, my lords."

"No," the magistrate agreed flatly. "You resigned your commission and came to London and decided that Rouge et Noir offered you a better chance than crop rotation?"

"I was very foolish, I know, sir, but Ned's loss came so unexpectedly, so soon after my father's . . . I had never thought to inherit. My talents are very different from Ned's. He was always conservative in seeking for solutions. I have always been a risk-taker."

"Taking risks is a strange talent," commented the magistrate sarcastically.

"Not in the army, my lords," Tony answered strongly. He'd be damned if he'd let them convict him without a fight.

"Yes, well, we have heard Colonel Bain and have seen several letters in evidence testifying to your bravery, that is true enough. So . . . you took to gaming to win back the family fortune, you lost heavily, you turned to Lady Fairhaven to bail you out. When she wouldn't continue to lend you money, you killed her in a fit of anger and desperation."

Tony's head came up. "That is an absolute lie, my lord. I . . . cared for Lady Fairhaven. I would never have harmed her."

"Are you calling this court a liar, Lord Ashford?"

"Not at all. I am, however, calling the charges lies."

"Do you deny that you were the last person to see Lady Fairhaven on the night of her murder?"

"I was the last to be seen with her, my lord. The last to see her would have been her murderer."

"Tell us about that last week, Lord Ashford." It was a soft, smooth, and kindly voice, and it came from the magistrate Tony had thought asleep. He still looked asleep, his hands folded over his stomach, his eyes half closed, but at least he sounded open-minded.

"Lady Fairhaven and I had become very close by then, my lords. Although nothing had been said yet, it was clear that when I proposed, she would accept. I asked her for a sum of money with which to pay off my debts and I promised that I would not go back to the tables."

There was silence. No short, sharp questions from this magistrate, so Tony continued. "I broke my promise, of course. Lost it all, sold some personal items, and won back three hundred pounds. I decided to go to Lady Fairhaven one more time. This time I was determined to stop gaming. I escorted her home that night. We were in the library. I confessed what I had done and asked her for another loan."

"Loan?"

"I asked her to help me pay off my immediate debts. She refused. I think it was at this point that her butler came into the library. I am sure he overheard our quarrel. But after she sent him up to bed, we talked further." Tony paused, seeing Claudia in front of him, remembering how humiliated he had felt, but also how sure he had been that this time he would be able to resist the call of the tables, how grateful he was to her for her generosity and love. But what good had that done Claudia . . . ?

The soft voice came again.

"Go on, Lord Ashford."

"It was a . . . difficult conversation, my lord. I had to admit that I was becoming a gamester— that I was letting my brother's hopes down. Letting her down. But by the end of it, she believed that this time I was sincere, and we had become betrothed. The notice was to have gone to the papers in the morning."

"And why would Lady Fairhaven have agreed to marry you, Lord Ashford?"

Tony hesitated. "Because she loved me, and knew I cared for her."

"You do not use the word 'love'?"

"I didn't love her in the same way. She knew that. But we both hoped I would come to love her."

"And?"

"I said good night and I left."

"With six hundred pounds."

"Yes. She had given me the money just before I said good night."

"And who let you out?"

"Jim. The under-footman." Tony's face brightened. "In fact, he would be a witness for me, my lords. I gave him a guinea and told him he was the first to wish me happy."

"How unfortunate, then, that this Jim has disappeared," commented the first magistrate in his most sarcastic of tones. "Who knows where he is, or indeed, *if* he still is."

"And after that you went straight home, Lord Ashford?" The second magistrate continued his soft questions.

"Yes, my lord. My valet can vouch for that."

"Where you were after the murder is hardly of interest to this court, is it, Lord Ashford?" asked his nemesis on the bench.

Tony just stood there silently, gripping the railing until his knuckles were white.

"What do you think happened after you left, Lord Ashford?" asked the quiet voice.

"I don't know, my lords. Perhaps Jim is the culprit, although he seemed very devoted to Lady Fairhaven. Or a common housebreaker. There have been a number of break-ins in the neighborhood recently. I only know that Lady Fairhaven was alive when I left."

"Wouldn't a housebreaker have been likely to have hit her with a heavy object? Or even strangled her?" The voice was still sympathetic.

"I would agree that that sounds most likely, my lord."

"And yet she was not strangled or killed in a painful manner. She was killed swiftly and in such a way as one might expect from a skilled soldier. Have you ever killed anyone in that particular way, my lord? By exerting pressure on the carotid arteries?" The magistrate's eyes opened slowly, and he leaned forward to hear Tony's answer.

Tony was silent.

"Have you, Lord Ashford?"

Tony let out a deep breath. "Yes, my lord, I have. Once. In Spain."

"Well, I think we have heard enough, don't you?"

The first magistrate nodded in answer to his colleague's question and Tony was led off, his mouth hanging open. That was it. He was a goner. He'd sit and rot in Newgate until the trial and then be convicted on the evidence. But there really *was* no evidence. Couldn't they see that? Why weren't they out looking for Jim? Why would he have wanted to kill Claudia for six hundred pounds instead of marrying her for thousands? And why in God's name hadn't he had the wit to say that?

He only had to wait a half hour before he was brought back.

"Anthony Varden, Lord Ashford, His Majesty's Court at Bow Street has decided that you are to be released," said the first magistrate. Tony started to shake uncontrollably.

The second voice continued, mellifluous as honey. As sweet as honey. "The evidence against you has been deemed largely circumstantial. And while the immediate motive, angry desperation, is convincing, it would seem you would have had a stronger motive to want Lady Fairhaven alive. At least, on the evidence before us. If, however, new evidence should appear against you, you will be immediately taken up. Have you anything to say, Lord Ashford?"

Tony had a hard time just getting out a "No, and thank you, my lords," through his chattering teeth. His hands were uncuffed and he realized that he was indeed free. He could go home and wash the smell of Newgate off him. He stumbled down the corridor and out the front door, feeling a mixture of euphoria and despair. He would send John to collect his few things from his cell. He could eat a decent meal. And he could prepare to return to Ashford. But he might as well throw his evening clothes and whatever invitations he might have received last week out the window. The court had judged him innocent. For now. But Claudia's murderer still went free. And until he was found and convicted, Tony Varden would be tainted by suspicion and shunned by society.

23

Joanna had sent a note to Gideon Naylor on the morning of the hearing, asking him to call on her afterward. By this time her parents were aware that she had hired a Runner and were reconciled to the fact, if not happy about it. It wasn't that they wanted her to abandon an old friend and neighbor. But there was something not quite respectable for a young woman to be paying for a man's defense, even if they had known each other for years. At any rate, her father had decided that it was more appropriate for the family to be funding Naylor, rather than Joanna herself.

When Gideon arrived, he was shown into the drawing room where Joanna sat with both her parents. After introductions, Lord and Lady Barrand left him with Joanna, having satisfied themselves that he was competent and not out to take advantage of their daughter.

"I am happy to tell you, Lady Joanna," said Gideon, "that Lord Ashford was released this morning."

Joanna, who had been sitting very straight, relaxed and gave Naylor a joyous smile. "Thank God, they saw he was innocent! However did you do it?"

"I have done nothing so far, Lady Joanna. The witnesses gave their evidence and the magistrates decided that there was not enough concrete evidence to bind Lord Ashford over for trial. For now."

"What do you mean, 'for now'?"

"He was very lucky Lady Fairhaven's will has not yet been read."

"Why?"

"Because could it be proved that Lord Ashford knew about it, it would provide a motive. I understand from her solicitor that he will benefit. By how much, I don't know."

"But he *is* free?"

"Oh, yes, he was free to go immediately. But since no one else has been arrested, Lord Ashford will still draw suspicion. An arrest always marks a man, you know. The public is always sure, unless there is absolute evidence to the contrary, that where there is smoke there is fire."

Joanna sighed. "I know you are right. Until we find the real criminal, Tony is ruined. Society is merciless, you know."

"Well, I have not given up all hope. In fact, I am rather optimistic," Naylor told her. "I have found out that Jim Tolin is really Jim Rooke and before Lady Fairhaven hired him, he was employed by Halesworth Limited."

"So Lord Fairhaven knew him?"

"Possibly. It seems too much of a coincidence to me. The young man's parents say that he was trained as a clerk to keep him out of service. The question is, why then did he end up as Lady Fairhaven's footman?"

"Perhaps he was an unsatisfactory clerk?"

"Perhaps. Or perhaps Lord Halesworth sent him into the household to act as a spy."

"Or Lord Fairhaven fired him and Jim is an unstable young man who wished to revenge himself on the family and killed Lady Fairhaven when she found him stealing from her," Joanna suggested, getting carried away by her scenario and convincing herself it was the answer.

Gideon smiled. "That is a possibility, certainly, but there has been no indication that Jim is in any way disturbed."

"How ever will you find him?"

"First, I intend to question Lord Fairhaven and some of his employees. Then it will be footwork," said Gideon, smiling again. "All those years in the infantry and I again am unable to put my feet up."

"When is Lady Fairhaven's will to be read?" Joanna asked thoughtfully.

"I believe not until next week, so I have some time to find this Jim."

"And is there really a possibility they could arrest Tony again?"

"If no other suspect is found, yes."

"Then, please God, you will succeed." Joanna stood up and extended her hand. "You will let me know as soon as you find anything?"

"Of course, my lady."

"And in the meantime, I will do whatever I can to salvage Tony's reputation," said Joanna, with far more optimism than she felt.

Joanna might have been able to summon some optimism in the afternoon, but after hearing the gossip flowing around her that evening, she realized how difficult her task would be. She made the effort to begin every conversation with a wide-eyed announcement of Tony's release. "Isn't it wonderful that they could find no evidence against Lord Ashford? It was disgraceful for a peer of the realm to be subjected to such treatment." It would hardly have been polite for her partners or acquaintances to disagree with her. And most of them did feel that an earl, no matter what the reason, did not belong in a public jail.

But Joanna's words were like stones in a stream. The gossip was halted for a moment, but then flowed on around them.

The next day she was hoping that Tony would call on her and was disappointed when the announcement never came. On one hand, she hadn't hired Naylor to earn undying expressions of gratitude, but on the other, a call from a friend to say "thank you" and let her know how he was faring wasn't too much to expect. She assumed she would see him that evening, but he was at none of the events she attended, which, of course, gave the gossips even freer rein.

She decided she was disappointed in him. He could have—no, he *should* have—called on her. And he certainly would have been wise to make an immediate appearance in society. His absence only made him look guilty. And so she asked her parents to send him an invitation to join them in a private supper and excursion to the theater the next evening.

"Are you sure you wish to do this, Joanna?" her mother asked.

"How can you say that, Mother? You have known Tony all his life. He needs every bit of support he can get. If old friends desert him, whom does he have?"

"I suppose you are right, my dear. It is only that a parent thinks of her own child first. I don't want you to suffer from your association with him. But yes, I will invite him," said Lady Barrand. "I am very fond of Tony too, you know," she added with a smile.

The invitation was returned with a polite refusal. Joanna was home alone when it was delivered and she was furious. Why was Tony being so stupid? She sat down and penned him a note, informing him that to refuse Lord Hunt was one thing, but to refuse old friends quite another. "If you will not come for your own sake, then please do so for the sake of my parents, who will be hurt by your refusal. If I do not hear in the affirmative," she added in a postscript, "I will have to come and persuade you in person."

She summoned a footman and sent him off, instructing him to wait for an answer.

Tony had spent the first hours of freedom soaking in a tub and letting the hot water relax him. He had sent his man out for spirits, and after he was out of his bath, had been shaved and dressed and splashed with lime-water cologne, he had put his heels up by his fire and drunk himself into a stupor.

He didn't awaken until noontime and was actually glad of the aftereffects of the last night's drinking. He would rather attribute his lethargy and depression to a hangover than think about the real reasons behind it.

John had placed a tray full of invitations in front of him when he sat down for coffee and a roll.

"Take them away, John."

"My lord, if I may be so bold—"

"You have never shrunk from it before, so I don't know why you hesitate now," said Tony with a smile.

"If you do not go out, people will be convinced of your guilt, despite the magistrates' verdict, my lord."

"Let them. If I do go, they will only avoid me or smile hypocritically while they turn down my invitation to a dance or supper. I wouldn't be surprised," said Tony, lifting one card and then dropping it back down into the pile, "if old Hunt refused me admittance entirely."

His valet gave up for the moment, knowing it would not work to push his employer when he was in this mood.

"What do you have planned for this afternoon, m'lord, so I can lay your things out?"

"Do I have any clothes left, John?" joked Tony.

"Enough to get by for a few days, my lord."

"Well, you may put out my buckskins. I'll ride this afternoon, before the crowds."

Tony's ride cleared his head. Other than pacing his little room at Newgate, he had had no real exercise for days. As he was leaving the park, he spied Colonel Bain coming in, and he guided his horse over, wondering what the response would be.

"Good afternoon, Colonel. I am greatly in your debt."

The colonel smiled and fell in beside him. "Nonsense. I was very happy to be a witness for you. It was ridiculous that they suspected you in the first place."

"I don't know, Bain. Now that I am free, I realize how reasonable their suspicions were, given the information they had. I was very fortunate."

"What are your plans?"

"Spend a few more days here, clearing off my immediate debts, and then taking myself back to Ashford. It is time I assumed my responsibilities."

"No more gaming? I am glad to hear that, Tony. Too many young men have been ruined at the tables."

"I think I have learned that lesson, Bain."

"We will miss you on the Continent, Captain Varden," said Bain, extending his hand as Tony began to turn his horse around.

Tony took it, grateful for the expressions of friendship and trust. "Thank you, sir," he said with a catch in his throat as he rode off.

Than evening, however, after he finished dinner and dismissed his valet, he wondered if he had learned his lesson. He had picked up one of the books Joanna had sent him, which John had brought back from Newgate. Unfortunately, it was Aurelius again. He had finished Miss Austen and supposed he was stuck with philosophy. But his attention would not stay on the page. All he could see in front of him were numbers, not words. "Thirty. One *après*." He could hear the calls, see the hands of the dealers as they turned the cards, feel the excitement at the table. He had the money back. The six-hundred pounds that the court had held had been returned. He could take a hundred pounds and spend a few hours at St. James Street. Surely a few hours would do no harm. And at least he knew he would be welcome there.

But he had promised Claudia. A promise he had intended to keep. But things were changed now. What did his promise matter, now that Claudia was dead? When there was no way but his brother's torturously slow solution to save Ashford. Why *not* spend a few hours in forgetting?

He sat there for a long time, the book forgotten in his lap, the struggle an internal one. Every time he was about ready to fling the old Roman into the fire, dress, and get the hell out of his depressing rooms, his depressing situation, he would see Claudia's face in front of him. She had believed in him and she had loved him.

But she's dead, so what possible difference does it make to her what I do? a part of him would say. And then he would see Joanna's face. His old friend who had the same faith in him, though only God knew why. Joanna had risked her reputation to visit him in that hellhole. Joanna had hired Naylor. How could he let either of the women down?

He finally fell into bed exhausted by the struggle and was surprised in the morning to see a ring of red welts on his right hand. Then he remembered that when the temptation was the strongest, he had bitten down on his hand almost hard enough to break the skin.

24

He got the Barrands' invitation that morning and sent back an immediate refusal. He couldn't imagine facing them, especially Joanna. He was deeply grateful to her, but was also very shamed that a woman to whom he was connected only by friendship had come to his rescue. And he had already decided that his withdrawal from society was the best course.

When he got Joanna's note, however, threatening to call on him if he didn't come to supper, he gave in. Damn her, he thought, ripping the note in half and throwing it in the fire, she would do it, too. Risk her reputation again for him. Why wasn't she a meek and mild little miss, this old friend of his, instead of such a strong-willed, stubborn woman? He fired a note back, accepting the dinner invitation only.

Joanna was relieved when she saw Tony's response, for she had been afraid she had gone too far. She dressed very carefully that evening, trying on one dress and then another, before settling on her apricot silk. This was so unusual for her that her abigail remarked upon it to the housekeeper: "After all, it is only Lord Ashford come for dinner, and my lady has known him from childhood!" The housekeeper said nothing aloud, but added to herself, *And loved him since then too, I would wager.*

At first, Tony wasn't sure whether the fact that it was only the family for dinner made it easier or more difficult. At first, they all uttered platitudes: "So glad to see you free, lad." "Happy to be so, sir." After all the polite nothings had been said, however, there was an uncomfortable silence at the dinner table until Tony broke it and finally opened the topic that was on all their minds.

"This is a meal made in heaven after Newgate fare, Lady Barrand."

"Was it really dreadful, Tony," she asked, reaching over and patting his hand.

"No. Well, yes," he admitted. "I was very lucky that I could buy my way into a private room. I hope I never have to see the place again."

"It is unlikely that you will, Tony," Joanna's father commented.

"The magistrates warned me that I could be arrested again were any further evidence found."

"Well, I have great hopes that Mr. Naylor will find something," said Joanna matter-of-factly, although her hands were shaking at the thought of Tony back in Newgate.

"I am ashamed I haven't thanked you all for hiring him," Tony said, flushing with embarrassment. "It was very difficult to accept such generosity."

"Nonsense," Lord Barrand answered. "We are old friends and neighbors. It is the least we could do. And besides, it was Joanna's idea, you know."

"Yes, I do know," Tony answered in a dead voice.

Joanna looked over at him. She had never given any thought to how Tony might experience her interference. She had acted immediately and from the heart. But men had very strange ideas about honor and pride, and she realized that although they were old friends, Tony might feel uncomfortable about being under such an obligation to her. All of a sudden she felt terrible. She had never wanted that. She had only wanted to help him.

"You had a report from Mr. Naylor, didn't you, dear?" asked Lady Barrand, very conscious of the sudden heavy atmosphere at the table.

"Yes. He has discovered the identity of the missing under-footman, Tony. Jim's real name is Rooke, and he was employed as a clerk at Halesworth Limited until a few weeks ago."

No matter what he felt about Joanna's interference, Tony could not help but be interested in such a piece of information.

"Surely Mark Halesworth would have known him, then? Has Naylor questioned him yet?"

"No. But that is his next step. As well as continuing his search for Jim."

Tony groaned. "The man could be anywhere in London."

"Maybe Halesworth will have some information," said Lord Barrand reassuringly.

When it was time to leave for the theater, Tony made it clear that he had no intention of making the Barrands a target for gossip.

"We invited you to fight the gossip, Tony," protested Joanna, with a touch of impatience in her voice.

"Perhaps I don't want you to help, Joanna," he said, so softly that her parents, who were on their way to the door, didn't hear. "And you risk your own reputation," he said, conscious that he had allowed his irrational resentment of her help to escape.

All the color left Joanna's face and then flooded back, as she first blocked and then felt the full impact of his remark. Her eyes flooded with tears and she had to quickly turn her face to avoid further humiliation.

Tony wished himself back in Newgate for his thoughtlessness. For the first time in all the years they had known each other, he had purposely wounded Joanna. He immediately realized that he had never even imagined she had the capacity to be hurt like this or that he had the power to do it. In a few seconds he had caught a glimpse of a vulnerable Joanna, a Joanna he had never known existed.

"Jo," he said hesitantly, reaching out to touch her shoulder, "I didn't mean that the way it sounded. I am very grateful for what you have done for me."

Joanna quickly wiped the tears off her cheeks and took a

deep breath before she turned and said in a low, fierce voice, "Well, I don't want your damned gratitude, Tony. I want—" She caught herself just in time. "I wanted to help you because it is what any old friend would wish to do for another." She smoothed her dress and stood up, becoming the old Joanna again, imperturbable, humorous, and self-contained. "Now, are you going to retreat, or are you going to take on the gossips as you took on the French?"

Tony smiled, relieved that his old Jo was back. "When you put it that way, my lady, what choice do I have?"

While Tony and the Barrands were taking on the *ton*, Gideon Naylor was sitting in the Garrick's Head drinking ale with a few of his out-of-work actor friends. He was basically a quiet man and enjoyed their company, for he could always count on their volubility. Indeed, by the end of an evening he could count on one or the other of them giving a fully declaimed monologue from one of his last roles. Naylor became their audience of one, and they played to him shamelessly. Occasionally they would push him to show one of the characters he used from time to time in his investigations, and they all agreed that he could have a career at the Drury Lane anytime he wanted to quit the Runners.

On this night, he was quieter than usual and seemed even a little distracted. Only a particularly dramatic rendering of Hamlet's third soliloquy, given by one of his friends to show that he, Robert Carthy, would have made a Dane superior to Kean's, that *he* would have gradually worked toward a grand crescendo, caught Naylor's attention.

"Well, you didn't have much crescendo in your Fortinbras, did you, Bob?" teased one of his companions.

Gideon sat there, letting it all flow around him, Hamlet's insight that "one can smile and smile and be a villain," repeating itself in his mind. Somehow it seemed important to his present case to remember that. What was Lord Ashford really like? Did his smile come from the inside, from genuine amusement, or was it only assumed? Did Lord Ashford "seem," or, like the Dane, did he "know not seem"?

Someone poked him in the ribs. "You are more than usually silent tonight, Gideon. Working on a new case?"

Gideon nodded. "A capital case," he replied. "The murder of Lady Fairhaven."

"The Fairhaven case? Didn't they already get Ashford for that?"

"I arrested Ashford," Gideon remarked with a modest smile.

"But I heard he got off," said Bob.

"Not enough hard evidence," admitted Gideon.

"What do you think, then, Gideon?"

"I try not to."

"Oh, no, here he goes again with his peculiar methods. We ought to call him a Bow Street Walker. Plod, plod, plod, and then, all of a sudden, inspiration, and our Gideon has solved the case!"

"Well, but he does solve some cases like that," Bob protested.

"I've walked miles already for this one, lads," said Gideon with a smile, as he got up from the table. "And I have miles more to cover, I'm sure. I'm off. I need my rest."

"Ah, homeward to a cold and empty bed. Farewell, Gideon."

"His bed is no colder nor emptier than ours."

"And that is the truth!"

Gideon turned at the door and looked affectionately back at his friends. They were good company, actors, and he was very glad of the proximity of Bow Street to Covent Garden and the theaters. His bed was usually empty until he himself climbed into it, and on nights like tonight when he was tired and lonely, it was good to distract himself by lifting a pint or two with his friends.

His rooms were only a few streets away. The house was clean, the rent reasonable, and the landlady a decent woman who had grown quite fond of her quiet lodger. Most of the time, Gideon was content with his chosen career and his cozy flat. But once in a while, like tonight, he wanted something more.

When he had returned from Portugal and gone home to Somerset, he had hoped that Mary Booth, with whom he had walked out a few times and from whom he had stolen a few kisses, might be waiting for him. But four years was a long time, and of course she had married. Not that they'd made any promises, but he was fond of her and had dreamed of her, and it did hurt, although he couldn't blame her in the least.

"I waited as long as I could, Gideon," she had told him as she stood there with a toddler clinging to her skirts and another one clearly on the way. "You were my favorite," she said with lowered eyes, "but Samuel and I are very happy."

Gideon had wished her well and not stayed around to embarrass her or himself. With his mother gone, and the rest of his family settled down and his old love unavailable, it was easy to see the city as a place of promise and a better future.

And so it had turned out to be, up to a point. He could never have stomached a job in service. Nor had he been drawn to factory work or farming. And after the army, he found he needed a certain amount of excitement to feel alive.

What he did was useful. The money was as good or better than anyone with his background could expect. But as he lay his head on the pillow, he wished there was someone beside him, someone to whom he could turn for encouragement and comfort. But what woman would be willing to share his life: out all hours, hobnobbing with the lowest criminals to get information, smelling of Newgate from time to time. No, it was just time to get himself a whore, he told himself as he drifted off. He would visit Mrs. Doyle's tomorrow night.

25

The next morning, after coffee and fresh rolls from the local baker, Gideon set out for the Fairhaven town house.

At first, the butler refused to inform Lord Fairhaven of his presence. "His lordship is very busy today and has no time for a caller without an appointment."

"I understand. But if you tell him it is Gideon Naylor from Bow Street, I am sure he will find a way to see me."

The man immediately became more respectful and went to deliver the message. He came back, looking a bit resentful at his employer's response, saying: "His lordship can see you now."

"Thank you." Gideon was amused at the man's annoyance. Servants to the rich and powerful often took on an air of self-importance that even outstripped their masters. He was used to it and used to the quick about-face when he identified himself. No one wanted to offend a Runner.

Lord Fairhaven was seated at his desk, going through the earl's correspondence. Gideon had to clear his throat to gain his attention, he was so absorbed. Or *seemed* so, thought Naylor. Now why did that word pop into his mind?

"Good morning, Mr. . . . . ?"

"Naylor, my lord. Gideon Naylor."

"Ah, yes. Please sit down. I have only a few minutes to give you," said Mark, waving his hand over his cluttered desk, "but of course bringing Lady Fairhaven's murderer to justice is of the greatest importance to me." Mark frowned.

"Not that I hadn't already thought he'd been caught. But I understand Lord Ashford was released yesterday."

"Yes, my lord," responded Gideon, sitting down on the other side of the desk. "The magistrates decided that there was not enough evidence: no witness to the crime, nothing left behind that would identify him."

"But what about his motive?" said Mark angrily. "He certainly had that. The man was desperate and Claudia had just refused him money."

"On the other hand, Lord Ashford states that he hoped to marry Lady Fairhaven. Indeed, that they became betrothed that night. That would certainly give him a motive to want her alive."

"He is lying. I don't think she ever would have married him. And I assume you received my note about Claudia's will. If Ashford were to benefit under that, then there is a strong motive."

"I was grateful for your information, my lord, and I did speak with Reresby. It does seem as though Lord Ashford will benefit, but it is not clear by how much, or if he knew about it."

"I wouldn't be surprised if Claudia was foolish enough to tell him," said Mark.

"Yes, my lord. It is possible." Gideon paused for a moment and then in his meekest and mildest of tones, said: "There is a curious fact that has just come to light, my lord, which is really why I came. It seems the under-footman who has disappeared from the Fairhaven household was not really an under-footman at all. Or Jim Tolin, for that matter. He is one Jim Rooke and up until a month ago was a clerk at Halesworth Limited." Gideon's face was at its blandest, his eyes seemingly sleepy and unfocused, but in reality, he was paying very close attention to Fairhaven's reaction.

Mark rubbed his hand over his face and gave Naylor a sheepish smile. "I have something to confess, Mr. Naylor."

"Indeed, my lord?"

"Jim was—or I should say is—one of my employees. He

was a bright young man, ambitious for promotion, to whom I offered a business proposition. I asked him to apply for that position in Claudia's household so that I could keep an eye on her. I was particularly concerned about her relationship with Ashford."

"And why would you decide to do that, my lord?"

"I have always been very fond of Lady Fairhaven, Mr. Naylor." Fairhaven's voice trembled a little and he glanced away as though it were painful to look Naylor in the face and talk about his feelings. "In fact, in the last two years, I realized that I cared about her a great deal. But she was very fond of my late cousin, and I intended to give her more time to recover her spirits before I would even consider approaching her as a possible suitor, much less pressure her. Tony Varden, on the other hand, was in desperate need of her money and had no other way to save his estate. I was afraid for Claudia. I didn't want to interfere in her life," continued Fairhaven slowly, "so much as just find out where things were at with Ashford. I hoped I could step in at the crucial point and dissuade her from marrying him."

"And so you introduced a sort of spy into her household?"

Fairhaven hesitated. "I suppose you might see it like that, although I didn't. Truly, I was only thinking of Claudia's future. How could I have known that I should have been worrying about her safety?" he added bleakly.

"And so you received regular reports from this Jim?"

"Yes."

"And what about the night of Lady Fairhaven's murder? Did you hear from him then?"

"No. I had been out at several events. It was late and I was tired, so I went directly home. I didn't hear about Claudia until late the next morning. And by then, Jim was gone."

"So he didn't run to you?"

"No. I must confess that I was surprised that he had disappeared. But when I think about it, the answer is obvious."

"Oh?" said Gideon, with a trace of irony.

"Of course, Mr. Naylor. Either Ashford threatened him and he is in hiding, or Ashford got rid of him too. I rather think the latter, don't you, Mr. Naylor, since he has not shown up?"

"It is certainly a possibility we have considered," admitted Gideon. "But I am still looking for him." Gideon got up out of his chair. "Indeed, I must be on my way. You will contact me should you hear anything from Jim, my lord?"

"Of course, Naylor, of course," replied Mark. "But I am afraid something has happened to him or he would have been to see me already." Fairhaven moved to the door of his office to open it for Gideon, all smiles and affability as he saw him out.

Mark watched until Gideon was halfway down the street before returning to his desk. He looked blankly at the letters he had been opening, his mind going around and around the question that had been plaguing him for days. Why *had* Jim disappeared? Why had he not contacted his employer? And the most terrifying question of all: Had he seen something that night, and was that the reason for his flight?

Gideon spent the day wandering the worst streets of St. Giles, seeking out his regular informants and giving them the usual incentives to keep their eyes open for a young man in footman's livery. After leaving Jim's description with half a dozen of his regulars, he suddenly realized that a fugitive, no matter how naive, might very well have decided to get rid of such noticeable clothes and headed for Petticoat Lane to question the old-clothesmen.

He hit five stalls before he found the right one. Yes, a young man had sold a suit of livery a few days ago, taking a used suit of clothes in return. Good news. But no, the owner of the stall had no idea where the young man was headed. The to-be-expected bad news.

So Gideon returned to St. Giles, tracked down his informants, and gave them the new information. On days like this, his job seemed impossible. Next he'd have to try the doss houses. Finding one man amongst all their customers would be like finding the proverbial needle in a haystack. And there was the whole city of London to hide in. And would a respectably reared young man have come here anyway? But you had to start somewhere, as Gideon well knew from previous cases, and so he visited numerous doss houses, ignoring the squalor and the smell and handing out pennies like candy to the ill-dressed urchins in the streets. He got home too tired to go to the pub, so he bought himself a pint and a pasty, and immediately after his solitary supper fell into bed, so exhausted that he had completely forgotten he had planned on female company for the evening.

26

The evening at the theater had been as bad as Tony expected. All eyes were on the Barrand box and all fans were aflutter in front of the ladies' faces as they turned to one another to exclaim upon the nerve of Lord Ashford and the foolishness of Lady Joanna in being seen with him.

During the interval only two people sought out their box: Colonel Bain, who purposely made himself very obvious by standing and chatting with Tony for almost the whole time, and Sir George Greene, a neighbor from Kent, who despite the protests of his wife had decided to show his support. "For I cannot believe that Ashford is capable of murder, my dear," he said to his wife, who only shook her head in despair and said, "Of course not, George, neither do I, but must you add us to the gossip?"

Tony was not surprised by the colonel's appearance, but he was very touched by the baronet's, whose standing in the *ton* was not very high. To risk a precarious status was very kind indeed, and Tony greeted him warmly while Joanna smiled her approval at Sir George. Later, she whispered to her mother that she hadn't believed he had it in him.

At the end of the evening, the Barrands dropped Tony off at his rooms. "You are going to attend Lady Howard's tomorrow, I trust?" Lord Barrand asked him.

"I had not intended to."

"Well, you must. You cannot let them think that they triumphed tonight."

"Lady Howard will probably have me turned away," said Tony, only half joking.

"Nonsense," said Lady Barrand.

"Are you sure you want to do this, my friends?" asked Tony very seriously. "It is one thing to invite me to a private dinner and attend the theater with me. Quite another to continue the connection and perhaps affect Joanna's chances. I would not like her to suffer for her admirable loyalty to an old friend."

Joanna leaned forward and looked out at Tony. "I am hardly a dewy young thing surrounded by admirers, Tony. I think I have enough consequence to carry it off. Any admirers I have will just have to take me as I am."

"Thank you, my lady," Tony replied, with a mock flourish and bow, trying to cover his sudden and, to him, surprisingly emotional response to Joanna's continuing loyalty.

As they drove away, Lady Barrand turned to her husband. "Do you think he will come?"

"Yes, I do. The boy is no coward and he owes Joanna something for all she has done for him."

"I have done very little, Father," said Joanna with a tinge of annoyance in her voice.

"Now, now, let us all just hope that all of this will blow over in a few weeks," said her mother soothingly.

"And that Gideon Naylor finds this missing footman," added Lord Barrand.

Joanna dressed very carefully for the Howard ball. Not, she told herself, to impress Tony. He never noticed her appearance anyway. But she wanted her gown to set her apart from the other young women. No spider gauze or white for her tonight. Instead, she chose a rather daring creation that she had not had the nerve to wear yet. It was made of a pale green Indian muslin shot through with gold thread. Green had always been her color, for it brought out the green flecks in her eyes. And the gold thread shimmered in candlelight. The bodice was cut lower than any of her other dresses, not scandalously, but enough so that she looked sophisticated.

Joanna was surprised when she gazed at herself in her pier glass. She looked—not beautiful, really, nor even pretty—but stunningly attractive all the same. She decided that she would make sure that Madame Celeste and she included more of this sort of gown the next time she went shopping.

She had always been very popular amongst men who enjoyed her refreshing, straightforward manner, but this evening she seemed to be drawing a few of those who obviously preferred more conventional female charms. She was pleased to shine, so that when Tony arrived—*if* he arrived— she would be seen to be squeezing him into her almost-full card, as anyone might do with an old friend, rather than seeking him out of pity or from a lack of partners.

She had almost given up expecting him when she heard him announced as she was being led off onto the dance floor. The ripple of surprise and disapproval that went over the assemblage was almost palpable to her, and she wondered if she should approach him immediately after this set. But this was a supper dance, she remembered and, she had already committed herself to her partner, so she could only hope that Tony was seeking out her parents or Colonel Bain.

She had a hard time concentrating on her supper plate or the conversation of her escort. She tried to nod at the appropriate times and interject polite little phrases, but all she could really think about was what was happening to Tony.

She was promised for the next country dance, but when her partner approached her, she smiled apologetically and asked if he would mind sitting it out with her. "I fear I overindulged at the refreshment table," she lied. Being at the edge of the ballroom gave her the opportunity to see where Tony had ended up. She was surprised to see him on the dance floor. Then, when she saw his partner, she understood. He had chosen, or perhaps it was the lady's doing, the wife of Lord Cathcart, who enjoyed living on the edge of scandal, never quite stepping over any lines that would have put her beyond the pale. Flirting with danger was how she survived marriage to a peer whom even his friends considered a monumental bore. Dancing with a possible murderer was just what Lady Cathcart would see as a challenge. Well, thank God there were women like her, thought Joanna with a combination of relief and jealousy.

When the music stopped, Joanna sent her escort off to his next partner, assuring him that she was fully recovered, and after he had disappeared, made her way toward Tony and Lady Cathcart.

She smiled brightly at them and complimented Lady Cathcart on her gown while Tony gritted his teeth in annoyance beside her. He had planned to dance with a few women who would enjoy the thrill of being partnered by someone on the edge, and then leave. He had not intended to seek Joanna out nor dance with her, but here she was, giving him no choice. He could hardly cut her, even for her own sake, so he smiled and chatted and wished he could wring her neck for exposing herself to scandal.

And exposing herself would seem to be the appropriate word, he thought, as he reluctantly admired her appearance. Her gown was not cut as low as Lady Cathcart's, but he had never seen quite so much of Joanna's bosom before, and he had to admit he liked seeing the way the line of freckles ended and the pale white skin of her breasts began. He hadn't realized her skin was so translucent. He heard Joanna speak to him, but couldn't really focus on what she was saying. His distraction surprised him. He had known Joanna for years. Why on earth was he noticing now how her slip clung to her figure under the pale green froth of her gown? He nodded his head and politely agreed to whatever she was saying when he suddenly realized she had been holding out her dance card and lamenting her lack of a partner for the next waltz. Apparently he had just agreed to save her from holding up the wall.

"You tricked me into that, Joanna," he growled into her ear as they moved onto the floor.

"I suspect it was the only way I could get you to dance with me," she replied.

"You are damned right, you foolish woman. I didn't want you to risk your reputation for me still again."

"You were just going to dance with a few upper-class whores like Lady Cathcart and then go home, is that it?"

Tony had to laugh. "You are incorrigible, Jo. You haven't changed a bit from the hoyden who attacked my shins. But I am glad you are still my friend," he concluded, relaxing for the first time that night and giving himself over to enjoying the waltz.

Usually he held Joanna very lightly and usually they chatted away together during a waltz. Tonight they both seemed to be mesmerized by the music and the practiced ease of their movements together. Tony was much more conscious of the slimness of Joanna's waist than he had ever been, and he found himself holding her a little closer and a little tighter than usual.

Tony's hand felt as if it were burning into Joanna's flesh as they whirled around, connected in a way they had never been before. She wished the dance would never end, but of course it did, all too soon. But as Tony escorted her off the dance floor and over to a group of her friends, he let his hand linger against her back a few minutes longer. It was very hard for her to smile naturally as he bowed his thank-you and moved away. She could feel the warmth of his hand against the small of her back for the rest of the evening.

Tony himself was surprised at how hard it was to make himself seek out Lady Cathcart for a second dance. He had wanted to stay with Joanna, gossip be damned. He had wanted to keep his arm around her waist and draw her close to him. It was the dress, he protested to himself. He just wasn't used to noticing Jo's curves. In fact, he hadn't realized until tonight that she had them.

* * *

Initially, Tony had given in to the Barrands' arguments because of friendship and his feeling of indebtedness to Joanna. He had intended no more than that private dinner and the theater, but then had been persuaded to attend the ball. He had promised himself that that would be enough. He would show his face, act as innocent as he indeed was, and then, having done his duty to friendship and the honor of his name, return to Ashford. If Bow Street wanted him for anything further, they could damn well come down to Kent.

But somehow he couldn't leave after the Howard ball. He told himself it was because he had made some progress against the gossip, and to leave London now would only make him look guilty or cowardly. He told himself a few more nights would do it. He told himself that Naylor might very well come up with the missing Jim in a few days and he wanted to be there when it happened. And all that he told himself was true. But he suspected that an additional reason was the memory of his waltz with Joanna. Somehow he couldn't stop thinking about her. Well, they were close friends, after all, he would tell himself. It was nothing more than that. But it was strange that for all the years he had known her he had never thought of her as an attractive woman before. He had only seen her as Jo, his boyish childhood companion, a friend who was like a sister to him. But surely he would not have wanted to hold a sister that close! He felt a combination of desire and shame, and he put it down to the effects of these last few weeks. He was vulnerable; he had lost Claudia, been arrested for murder, spent time in prison. That was the reason for these unfamiliar feelings. And Joanna *was* an attractive woman, although he hadn't paid much attention to the fact before. His response was a natural one. At any rate, he didn't want to do anything that would threaten their friendship. But he would stay a little longer in London, because surely that was the wisest thing to do.

* * *

Joanna had felt the change in Tony and couldn't help herself from hoping that something had shifted between them. They had shared so much over the years. Surely Tony's response meant that he was finally recognizing her as a woman. She went home and dreamed of him all night and moved through the next day in a fog. Surely he would dance with her again, hold her close again. But although he did ask her to dance the next night, it was only for a country dance and a cotillion. And he did not seek out any opportunity to be private with her. He was the same old Tony. Almost. And that small difference Joanna could put down to the vulnerability of his situation.

When he showed up a third night at a supper dance and only partnered her once, Joanna began to think she had only imagined the moments of attraction between them. Or perhaps he just didn't need her anymore, she thought, with a cynicism quite foreign to her nature. Although he was receiving only half the invitations he normally would have and had been cut regularly, although not universally, his regular appearances were beginning to impress those who had had some doubts all along. Surely a man who was guilty of murder would not have the nerve to face continual set-downs? No mothers would let their young daughters near him, but several respectable widows and matrons accepted his invitations to dance, and more than a few of his acquaintances, who had ignored him rather than cut him directly, were letting themselves be drawn back into his company.

All in all, he was quite the social success for an accused murderer, thought Joanna rather bitterly. She knew she was being unfair to Tony. He was acting no differently than he ever had to her. It was just that there had been that one night when something wonderful flowed between them. She supposed she had only imagined it.

27

While Tony Varden was making his way back into society, Gideon was still tramping the streets. None of his usually reliable informants had seen anyone resembling Jim, and he wondered if concentrating on this one area, although it was the easiest place in London for someone to hide, was wasting time.

Usually he would have had some breakthrough in a case by now: either a piece of information or an inspiration. He usually solved his cases, as his actor friends had said, by a combination of painstaking investigation and a flash of intuition. The thorough inquiries seemed to keep his mind occupied so it didn't interfere with his seemingly irrational ability to suddenly see the way to a solution in a case.

The only stirring of intuition in the Fairhaven murder, however, had occurred when he had visited the present earl. Something was not quite right there, he was sure. Fairhaven's explanation for placing Jim in his cousin's household was too pat. And although Fairhaven was rich, some people could never have enough money. Despite a bequest to Ashford, Fairhaven would benefit greatly from Lady Fairhaven's demise. And so Gideon desperately needed to find this elusive Jim.

After another two days in the rookeries and doss houses and two nights of falling into bed exhausted and alone, he decided it was high time for some female company. He never employed any of the whores around Covent Garden, for that was too close to his job and his home. Instead, he had discovered a small, well-run brothel where he had two special "friends." If Grace was busy then Annie was usually available for him. Once, in fact, when Grace was slowly and exquisitely bringing him to a climax, Annie had slipped into the room and he had spent the rest of the evening enjoying both of them. He smiled at the memory. But that had been a few years ago, when he was younger and not so leg-weary.

He was surprised when his knock was answered by one of the neighborhood urchins tricked out in footman's livery, but assumed it was a new ploy to compete with other houses in the area by looking more respectable. It wasn't until he had spent several delightful hours with Annie, who was as adept at back and foot rubs as she was with stroking other parts of his anatomy, that he thought to comment on it.

"Hit does look a bit ridiculous, doesn't hit?" she said laughingly as Gideon stroked her hair and cuddled her to him.

"Why a footman? Surely Mrs. Doyle isn't losing business with girls like you and Grace in her house."

"Not really, but she 'eard about Mrs. Spencer's 'iring one. They've known one another for years—started in the same 'ouse together, or so I've 'eard—and 'ave always been friendly competitors."

"So Mrs. Spencer hired a budding young criminal first, eh?"

"No, I ain't seen 'im but I've 'eard 'e's a proper footman, all right. Mrs. Doyle is furious, because she couldn't find anyone like 'im, who'd really been in service."

Gideon was so relaxed that it almost went right by him. He was not thinking about his case, but about how delightfully rounded Annie's bottom was, and how it fit so well against him, and how her roundness was making his desire stir again, when what she was saying finally penetrated.

"You say he's actually been in service? A proper footman?"

"'E's very himpressive, I've been told, Gideon," said Annie, rubbing her bottom against him.

"When did she hire him? Is he a young man?"

"I don't know 'ow old 'e is. But she only got 'im a few days ago."

"Where did you say Mrs. Spencer's was?"

"On Buckwall Street. You aren't leaving already, Gideon? You aren't going to desert Grace and me for Mrs. Spencer's just because she's 'ired some posh footman are you?" asked Annie plaintively. She would hate to lose Gideon as a customer. So would Grace. He was one of the few who actually seemed to see them as women, not just whores. He would hold them and talk to them, not just rush off after she or Grace had done them.

Gideon patted her shoulder reassuringly. "Now how could I desert you and Grace, Annie? You give such expert . . . back rubs!" They both laughed. "No, this is business. You may have given me some information that will save me a few days' walking."

Gideon left an extra coin on the nightstand and let himself out, leaving Annie to look wistfully after him. Aside from the nights she spent with Grace, cuddling up to Gideon helped keep her feeling human.

It was late, but Gideon was used to these streets at night and feeling rested, so he decided to walk. Sometimes, when the illusion of having an affectionate sex partner that Grace and Annie gave him faded, he wished he really had a woman in his life, not just two whores who pretended to care about him. Well, maybe not pretended. He thought he could safely say they liked him. He certainly felt some affection for them. And they were clean, at least he knew that about them. No, he was lucky to have Grace and Annie and foolish to want more. After all, what decent woman would spend her life with a Bow Street Runner?

He reached Buckwall Street sooner than he thought he would. Mrs. Spencer's was a bigger house than Mrs. Doyle's, and from the outside at least, appeared more prosperous. As he started toward the door, it opened and he saw a young man in footman's livery helping a departing customer with his coat. It was hard to tell from the street, but he seemed to fit the general description of Jim. Gideon stepped back to let the departing man by, and then walked up to the door.

"Is this Mrs. Spencer's?"

The footman's demeanor and response were as formal as if he were admitting a duke to a Mayfair town house rather than a customer into a brothel.

"Yes, sir. Who may I say is calling?"

Gideon grinned. Mrs. Spencer was certainly after a higher class of customers for her girls than the usual small bawdy house.

"Tell her Gideon Naylor."

The young man motioned him into the parlor and went to get his mistress. As Gideon waited, he looked around with his usual curiosity, a combination of professional habit and a natural interest in people.

The room was tastefully decorated with Turkey carpets and attractive prints hanging on the walls. He was looking at one of these when the door opened behind him.

"Mr. Naylor?"

Gideon turned and saw a tall woman enter. She was dressed in a burgundy-red silk gown cut low over her bosom. Her black hair—a little too black to be natural, thought Gideon—was caught up into a Psyche knot and her face was carefully and tastefully made up. Her nose was rather aquiline and her brown eyes hard, but her mouth was full and soft and at odds with the rest of her features. Gideon guessed they were close in age, and realized as she stepped forward that they were about equal in height.

"You are Mrs. Spencer?"

"Blisse Spencer," she said with a practiced smile, holding out her hand.

Gideon took it and held it for a moment.

"How may I help you, Mr. Naylor?"

"I have just come from Mrs. Doyle's."

The woman's eyes narrowed, but her smile didn't change. "A very satisfactory house, Mr. Naylor. I know

Mrs. Doyle. But I pride myself in thinking that mine is even more comfortable."

"It would certainly appear so, Mrs. Spencer. Your footman is certainly far superior," said Gideon with a smile.

Mrs. Spencer gave him a genuine smile at that observation. "Yes, I have walked by and seen her new . . . employee. We have been friendly rivals, you see, and as soon as I hired Jim, she had to go and get herself someone. Now, what can I get you, Mr. Naylor? A brandy? Champagne? A room for a few hours?"

Gideon shook his head. "I have had enough to drink tonight, Mrs. Spencer. And Annie—you perhaps know Annie— has quite satisfied my other needs."

"Then why are you here, Mr. Naylor? Surely not just to compare the quality of our footmen."

"Actually, that is precisely why I am here."

Mrs. Spencer frowned and was about to get up when Gideon put out his hand and took her wrist. His grasp was gentle but firm, and she sank back down in her chair.

"I am a Runner, Mrs. Spencer. And also a regular customer at Mrs. Doyle's," he added with a quick grin. "I have been looking for one Jim Rooke for days, and when Annie described your footman I suspected I might have found him. I want you to tell me what you know of him."

"Nothing," Mrs. Spencer replied coldly. "I hired him off the street."

"Now, Mrs. Spencer. Blisse, did you say? Why would you have hired a young man without knowing anything about him? You seem a shrewd woman, Blisse. I can't quite fathom you doing that."

"I am Mrs. Spencer to you, Mr. Naylor. And whether you fathom it or not, it is true."

Gideon was sure there was more to it than she was telling him, but he decided to let it go for the moment. After all, he wasn't here to harass Mrs. Spencer, but to find Jim. Which he was sure he had done.

"Perhaps you would be interested in hearing that your new employee is wanted in a murder case?"

Mrs. Spencer responded coolly that she found this hard to believe, but if a Runner of Mr. Naylor's obvious stature said so, than it must be true.

Gideon ignored the sarcastic emphasis she placed on "stature" and said: "I think we will have Jim in. No, no please don't get up, Mrs. Spencer. I will summon him." Gideon suspected that the woman would have warned Jim off, and so he opened the parlor door and told the young man that Mrs. Spencer wanted to see him. Gideon shut the door after him and stood in front of it.

28

As Jim approached Mrs. Spencer, she just waved her hand in Gideon's direction. Jim turned to him, and then glanced back at his employer with a puzzled look on his face. "Should I show the gentleman up to a room, madam?"

"No, Mr. Rooke. That is your name, isn't it?" asked Gideon with an assumed air of innocence.

Jim fought hard to keep himself from bolting past Naylor and out the door. He was silent, not sure how he had been found or by whom. If this was another employee of Lord Fairhaven's, he would not say a word. But surely Lord Fairhaven would have sent someone bigger and more dangerous-looking.

"Mr. Naylor is a Bow Street Runner, Jim," Mrs. Spencer announced.

Jim didn't know if he was more relieved or terrified. Thank God Fairhaven hadn't found him. But if the Runners were after him, what did that mean and what chance did he have? In fact, Fairhaven himself could have hired a Runner to find him, he suddenly thought, the fear rising again.

"I have been hired by Lady Joanna Barrand to investigate Lady Fairhaven's murder. She is an old friend of Lord Ashford's, who was arrested for the crime."

"Lord Ashford?" Jim repeated, a look of surprise on his face.

Interesting, thought Gideon. He didn't seem to expect that name.

"Anthony Varden, Lord Ashford. From what we know so

far, he was the last person to see Lady Fairhaven alive. Of course," Gideon added sarcastically, "we were missing one key witness. Yourself. Or were we missing the murderer?" he continued in a deceptively friendly voice.

Jim started. "Me? Kill Lady Fairhaven? Oh no, sir, never!"

"You were a very new employee, after all. It is odd, Mr. Rooke. You seem to be quite adept in finding short-term service in, ah, various sorts of houses. Did Mark Halesworth send you here too?"

Jim's shoulders slumped. "So you know," he whispered.

"I know that Lord Fairhaven wanted a spy in the household and that you were hired to be that spy. I know that you may have opened the door to Lady Fairhaven's killer. I am just not quite sure who that killer was."

Mrs. Spencer, who had been watching very closely, marveled at Naylor's technique. His tone was even, his voice low—so low she almost had to stop breathing at times to catch what he was saying. His personality, what she had seen of it, receded like his hairline, so that the space between the questioned and questioner was all taken up by Jim's fear. There was no contempt or anger in Naylor's voice. There was nothing but mild interest. How skillful, she thought. If he had bullied, Jim would have bolted or resisted, she was sure. Instead, he pulled himself out of the way and left all the space for Jim. *How would he have handled me?* she wondered, and then realized that she was as curious about him personally as professionally.

Jim swallowed several times. "Lord Ashford was actually arrested for the murder?"

"Yes."

"But he is not likely to be convicted, sir? A peer of the realm, and all?"

Naylor decided not to tell him that Ashford was free for the moment. "We have a witness—the butler—who heard him quarreling with Lady Fairhaven. We have a motive: six hundred pounds. Perhaps even a larger motive; we won't know until her will is read. Peer of the realm, or no, he will swing if he did it."

Jim was desperate. He didn't want Ashford condemned for a crime he didn't commit. But neither did he want to risk his own safety. If he came forward, what would stop Fairhaven from having him killed before the trial?

"Of course, if we had a witness, someone who saw Ashford leave and Lady Fairhaven still alive, well, then, he would be in no danger, would he?" said Gideon mildly.

Maybe there was a way out, thought Jim. Naylor was giving him refuge, not pushing him out into the cold. All he had to admit to was Lady Fairhaven's appearance at the library door, asking him to let Lord Ashford out, and Lord Ashford's announcement of their betrothal. That would clear Ashford without implicating him or Lord Fairhaven. He let his breath out in a deep sigh and told Gideon the partial truth.

"And you are sure that Lady Fairhaven was alive when Ashford left?"

"Oh, yes, sir," said Jim, relieved and happy.

"And Ashford told you about their betrothal?

"He was very happy and generous, sir. He gave me a guinea."

"So you did have some money when you ran?"

"Uh, yes."

"But what I still do not understand, Jim," said Gideon softly, "is *why* you ran."

Oh, dear, thought Mrs. Spencer. *He has him now.*

"Uh, you see, sir, I was feeling more and more unhappy about my position in the house, sir. Lady Fairhaven was very kind to me. It was beginning to feel wrong to be spying on her. And if they were already engaged . . . well, then, my job was over anyway, wasn't it? So I left."

"But you didn't return to Halesworth Limited? Didn't report to Lord Fairhaven?"

"Well, er, no, sir. I thought he would be annoyed with me, leaving my post and all. And I wasn't all that happy, being a clerk."

"So you thought to better yourself, is that it, and took on a position in a whorehouse?"

"It was the best job I could find, sir. Mrs. Spencer was very generous with me," he said stoutly.

Mrs. Spencer stood up and approached them. "Yes, Jim has added a certain cachet to my house which it didn't have before. The customers quite like it, and indeed, I am drawing in a better class as the word spreads. Now, I am sure you would like to take down Jim's statement, Mr. Naylor, so he can get back to work. I will be right back with pen and paper."

"Sit down, Jim," Gideon said firmly.

"Yes, sir."

"I assume you are willing to write out a statement?"

"Absolutely, sir. I wouldn't want an innocent man convicted."

"And what about the guilty one, Jim? What of him? Would you want him convicted?"

"Of course, sir. If I knew who he was."

And something tells me you do, Jim, said Gideon to himself. But he also knew that the boy was terrified. He had come up with a halfway decent story on the spur of the moment, but it was obviously a lie. His parents would die if they knew where he was, and from all reports, he was very close to them. No, he had run in fear that night, and was in hiding here. Well, if he was that scared, he probably had good reason for it, and Gideon wasn't about to have his star witness killed before he could give testimony.

Mrs. Spencer was back with a few sheets of vellum and a pen, and Jim, in his clear and painstaking clerk's hand, wrote a detailed account of that evening. After it was sanded and folded, Gideon put it in his coat pocket.

"I am grateful for your cooperation, Jim. As will be Lady Joanna and Lord Ashford. And thank you for your unwilling help, Mrs. Spencer," he added with an ironic smile. "Jim, you seem quite happy in your employment here. I would advise you not to go anywhere until the real murderer is apprehended. You should be safe here. It is unlikely that Annie will be entertaining anyone else interested in you. I have enjoyed meeting you, Mrs. Spencer. I will be stopping by from time to time, to check on Jim. Who knows, maybe I will grow to like it and change my custom from Mrs. Doyle's to here."

"You would be most welcome," said Mrs. Spencer, with a smile that did not reach her eyes.

29

Gideon Naylor's visit had shaken Mark Halesworth. He had not expected anyone to make the connection between him and his ex-clerk. In fact, he had not expected much investigation at all. Ashford had the strongest motive, after all, and there was a witness to implicate him. Jim's disappearance was disturbing, but unless he reappeared, Mark could continue to throw suspicion on Tony Varden.

But now that the Barrands had hired themselves a Runner, there was a possibility that Jim might be found. A slight possibility, of course. But who would have thought that the unprepossessing Naylor would have been able to trace Jim back to Halesworth Limited.? If Gideon Naylor did succeed in finding Jim, then Mark wanted to be sure he knew about it.

He decided to have Naylor followed. And he had just the man to do it: Tom Drabble, who was one of his employees on the docks.

The day after Naylor's visit, therefore, he left the office early and made his way to the dockside. He was in mourning, and was almost invisible as he stood in the shadows, waiting for the men to leave. Drabble was one of the last, and luckily for Mark, he was alone. He emerged from the alley long enough to beckon him over.

"Mr. 'Alesworth! Oi mean, Lord Fair'aven. Wot a surprise to see you 'ere, m'lord." Drabble was a small, weasel-faced man whom Mark had hired for odd jobs before, usually to spy on his fellow workers, to make sure none of them lifted any Halesworth goods."

"I have a job for you, Drabble."

"'Oo is it this time, m'lord? Someone in the warehouse?"

"Actually, you are going to take a few days off, Drabble. I want you to do a little following for me."

"Following, m'lord?"

"Yes. And I will pay both your wages and your usual rate."

Drabble sniffled. It was an unpleasant habit he had, and Mark was always tempted to hand him a handkerchief. His long nose was always dripping and, indeed, his fellow workers had dubbed him Tom Dribble. Thank God he did not have to use his nose to find anyone, thought Mark, as he watched Drabble wipe it on his sleeve. Were he a hound, he'd be completely useless in picking up a scent. But he was surprisingly good at sniffing out the thief in the warehouse or picking up news on the street about Mark's competitors.

"'Oo will Oi be following, m'lord?"

"Actually, Drabble, you'll be following a Bow Street Runner."

"A Runner, sir?"

"One Gideon Naylor."

"Naylor!"

"You've heard of him?"

"'Oo 'asn't? 'E's one of the best thief takers they've got."

"He didn't strike me as very threatening."

"No, 'e doesn't, and therein lies 'is strength, m'lord." Sniffle, sniffle.

"Do you think you can stay close to him without him knowing it?"

"Oi think so, sir. Oi'm werry good at wot Oi do too."

"Indeed, you certainly are. I particularly want to know if and when Naylor comes across a certain young man, Jim Rooke. Be on him first thing in the morning."

"Yes, sir. Oi'll plant meself at Bow Street and start from there."

"And you are sure he won't notice you?"

"Oi think not, my lord."

"I don't want any connection made between us, Drabble. I'll meet you at the Golden Crown for a report in the next few days."

Sniffle. "Yes, m'lord."

"Be off with you, then. I don't want anyone seeing us together." Mark could hear Drabble snuffling his way down the street. He might sound ridiculous, but he was good, and if Naylor found Jim, Mark was sure that Drabble would only be a few yards behind.

The next morning Drabble was at his post near the magistrate's court. When Gideon emerged, he only went as far as the Garrick's Head, where he sat himself down to a plate of ham and eggs and a large tankard of ale. He looked relaxed and not as though he were on a job at all, thought Drabble, who was standing at the bar, waiting for the bartender to pull him a glass of beer. Drabble drank slowly, and when Gideon got up, turned his back to the door. But he finished his beer quickly and was out in time to see Naylor turn the corner. He sauntered after him and watched him approach a cabstand. Damn. Fairhaven hadn't said anything about expenses, so he would have to spend some of his wages to follow. He was lucky he was close enough to overhear Naylor's destination.

Drabble told his driver to drop him off two streets further and they passed Gideon's cab just as the Runner was going up the steps of 15 Clarges Street. Drabble ignored the grumbling about "cheap bastards wasting a driver's time." He wasn't about to add anything to the cab fare. Not if the expenses might be on him.

He walked back to Clarges Street and wondered how he could find out on whom the Runner was calling. It had to be business, because Naylor was unlikely to be paying social calls in this neighborhood.

* * *

While Drabble was waiting, Gideon was giving Tony the good news.

"You actually found him, Naylor? Sit down, sit down and have a cup of tea with me."

"No, thank you, my lord. I've had my breakfast already," said Gideon, pulling up a chair.

"Did Jim confirm my story?" asked Tony eagerly.

"Yes, my lord. In fact, I have a signed statement from him right here in my pocket."

"Which you will give to the magistrate immediately, I hope."

"Well, my lord, that is why I am here. You are in no immediate danger of being picked up again. At least not until after the will is read," Naylor amended. "I don't want it generally known that the footman has been found."

"Why not?" demanded Tony.

"Because he may be in danger. I persuaded him to write this statement by appealing to his sense of justice. He did not want to have an innocent man convicted. But I have a very strong feeling that he knows who the guilty man is and is hiding from him."

"Didn't you question him? Surely you can make him tell you. You must have methods of getting people to talk." Tony didn't feel so desperate now that Naylor had found someone to confirm his story, but he was anxious to find out the whole truth. Only finding the murderer would avenge Claudia's death and clear him completely in the eyes of society.

"We all have our preferred methods, my lord," Gideon answered. "I adjust mine to the circumstances. And the person."

"So I have heard. 'Mild with the mild, terrible with the terrible.'"

Gideon smiled. "Jim does not need to be terrified. He already is. No, I will go back tomorrow and make sure he is still safe and ask a few more questions."

"Where *did* you find him?"

"He is employed as a footman in a bawdy house, my lord."

Tony choked on his muffin. "How ever did you discover that?" he asked, after the paroxysm of coughing had stopped.

"You could say I have my sources, my lord," Gideon replied with a quick grin.

"I see," Tony said with a smile. "Maybe I should meet your sources, Naylor. Just to see if they are reliable, of course."

"I am sure you have your own, er, sources, my lord, in far better neighborhoods."

"Yes, but I must confess that I have been short on both money and desire lately."

"I know what that can be like."

"I miss Claudia, you know," admitted Tony. "She was a good friend. Not," he immediately added, "that she was anything more to me. I mean, I cared for her, but we had done nothing more than kiss. I must be overcome with relief, Naylor," said Tony with a sheepish smile. "I don't know why I am telling you all this. Except that I am lonely."

"But you have another good friend in Lady Joanna."

Tony sighed. "Yes, I do. But I have been avoiding her."

Gideon looked puzzled.

"For her own sake. And perhaps a little bit for mine. I find I am beginning to see her differently."

"How so, my lord?"

"Not just as a friend. But I am sure she feels nothing like that for me. I will just have to look up one of my own 'sources.' Then I will be less blue-deviled."

Gideon, of course, was sure that friendship, no matter how deep, was not all that was behind Lady Joanna's actions. But who was he to tell Lord Ashford that?

"I am off to Lady Joanna's right now, as a matter of fact, to give her my report."

"And that will be that. I can't thank you enough, Naylor.

At least I am no longer in danger of hanging, even if half of society ignores me."

"I have done what Lady Joanna hired me to do, my lord. But I hate to stop . . . I'd continue if . . ."

"If someone hired you to?"

"Yes, my lord."

"And how much do you charge, Naylor?"

"A guinea a week and expenses."

"Well, I could afford that for a short while. Why don't I hire you and see what you come up with before I return to Ashford? The least I can do for Claudia is try to find her murderer."

"Thank you, my lord. I welcome the opportunity to continue my investigation."

Tony put his hand out and Naylor shook it. "Good luck, Naylor."

Drabble, who was leaning against the fence across the street, watched Naylor come out. To his great relief, Naylor did not go near a cabstand, but proceeded to walk to Berkeley Square. He was clearly headed for another *ton* household. And when he stopped at Number 10, Drabble drew back into an alley as Naylor stood on the steps, waiting to be admitted.

Joanna was delighted with Gideon's news.

"This means that Tony is unequivocally cleared, doesn't it?"

"Yes, my lady. As soon as I hand the statement over to the magistrates."

"Which you will do today, I assume?"

Gideon explained his decision to delay and Joanna nodded thoughtfully.

"Yes, I can see that you wish to protect your witness. And you think that he is concealing the identity of the real murderer?"

"I am sure, my lady."

Joanna sat quietly for a moment and then looked over at

Gideon. "Mr. Naylor, I would like you to continue working for me . . . for us. That is, I am sure my father will agree that we shouldn't end the investigation until we have found the guilty man."

"I would like to accommodate you, my lady, but I have already been retained by someone else."

"Oh, no, you can't give this up now that you are so close," protested Joanna.

"Well, I am not exactly giving up, my lady," Gideon told her. "It is Lord Ashford who has hired me."

"Tony?"

"Yes. I believe he feels very strongly about bringing Lady Claudia's murderer to justice."

"Of course," said Joanna, after a moment. "And I suppose it is more fitting. I am just . . . surprised. I didn't think he had the money."

"The money Lady Fairhaven had given him was returned to him upon his release."

"Of course." Joanna thanked Gideon for his efforts, insisted on giving him a guinea bonus, and wished him well in his further investigation. After he left, she found herself standing before the French doors that opened onto their small garden. If she was so pleased that Tony had been vindicated, why was she feeling so disappointed? It had felt good to be able to do something for Tony. Now that special connection with him was broken. She hadn't done it to gain his attention and gratitude, of course, but they had been the by-products of her action, nevertheless. Now she would resume her place in the background of his life. And Claudia was still somehow in the forefront . . .

How despicable, she told herself, to resent a dead woman. And how uncharacteristic of Tony to take on a responsibility like that. She was as surprised as disappointed. Joanna was nothing if not as honest with herself as she was with others. She was always bemoaning the fact that Tony only saw her as his steadfast, commonsensical old friend Joanna. But how had she been viewing him? It seemed that she had only allowed him a limited role. He was the volatile, dashing, risk-taking soldier. Responsible in his chosen career, but incapable of settling down and assuming everyday responsibilities. And for years she had been infatuated by and critical of that Tony Varden.

But this Tony was taking things out of her hands and into his. She should be pleased, shouldn't she? Then why did she feel that her world was beginning to shift?

30

Gideon had decided that half his bonus would be well spent on a round of drinks for his friends, a good dinner, and a night in the arms of Annie or Grace. Drabble followed him home and a few hours later watched him emerge in his second-best suit of clothes and walk to the Garrick's Head. Drabble took a table in a dark corner, and ordered himself something to eat and drink as well, since it looked as if Naylor would be there for a while. This part of the job was not burdensome, he thought, as he sniffled and use the napkin as a handkerchief.

At some point in the evening, when the drinks had been flowing for an hour or so, one of the actors leaned over the table and tugged at Gideon's sleeve.

"Gideon, my love, mark that weasel-faced bloke in the corner. Now he would be a fine character for you to assume someday. Sniffling and snuffling around with that long nose of his." Bob, who was more than a little cast away, slid his hand down Gideon's arm and grasped him by the hand. He looked up at Gideon with bleary eyes and said: "Ah, and would that you were my love, Gideon."

Gideon smiled. About every three months, Bob would get very drunk and confess his attraction. Gideon would give him a sweet smile, repeat his unfortunate, in this instance, predilection for the female of the species, Bob would shed a few tears and then fall asleep at the table.

"Wouldn't you think he would have given this over by now," said one of Bob's friends. "Good thing you don't get put off by it, Gideon."

"I don't mind." Nor did he. Gideon figured affection and good fellowship were hard to come by in his world, or in any world, for that matter. He knew Bob's little ritual was only that, and hardly a sign of a broken heart. Gideon's best friend in the 47th Foot had preferred men, and it had never presented a problem, either in their friendship or their soldiering.

He got up shortly thereafter and bade them all good-bye. "I am off, boys. I wish you luck tomorrow. I am sure a part is certain to turn up." This was Gideon's little ritual, to wish his friends employment. Not that they regularly found it, of course. The group at the Garrick's Head was continuously shifting, as one actor was hired and another let go.

He was feeling very mellow tonight and strolled slowly and seemingly unconsciously through the streets. No matter how much he had drunk, however, he never lost his sensitivity to his surroundings. He turned several times, thinking he had heard someone behind him, but decided it was only a rat scurrying away.

Mrs. Doyle greeted him and told him it would be Annie again tonight, since Grace was otherwise occupied. "But it will be a short night, Gideon, given the hour and the fact that Annie has an early-morning customer."

Maybe it was because he had to leave sooner than he would have liked, or maybe it was because he had had more to drink than usual, but Gideon found himself noticing the practical efficiency of Annie's lovemaking. Usually he was taken with her blowzy blond charms, but this night he found himself wondering what it would be like to have the ever so businesslike Mrs. Blisse Spencer in bed with him. He laughed at himself. Mrs. Spencer was clearly a hard-eyed businesswoman, and no doubt would be even more efficient than Annie. But the memory of her soft, full mouth kept intruding, and he decided that he needed to check on Jim's safety very soon. Maybe even tomorrow night.

The next morning, during a late breakfast, Gideon decided that another visit to Lord Fairhaven was in order. The more he thought about it, the more he was convinced that despite Fairhaven's sizable fortune, he was the most likely suspect. As he drank his coffee, he let his mind relax and tried to imagine what it would be like to be Mark Halesworth. He had been his cousin's closest male relative, in line for both title and fortune for years. Since the late Lord Fairhaven had not married until he was forty-seven, Mark must have grown up expecting both as his due. And then, suddenly, the marriage to Lady Claudia and the possibility of an heir. He would have watched and waited and perhaps even hated Lady Fairhaven. And when no heir seemed to be forthcoming, wouldn't he have started to hope again? After his cousin's will, he must have at least considered the possibility of marriage with the widow. Then along came Tony Varden. Lord Fairhaven had the title, but he most certainly would have finally lost the fortune forever, had Lady Fairhaven remarried and had children.

It was an odd thing, thought Gideon, as he came out of his reverie. To the judges and to most observers, Tony Varden had the strongest motive because he was in such desperate need for immediate funds. It seemed obvious: the man most in need was the man who would be driven to crime, which was certainly often true. But Gideon had seen too much in his years as a Runner to dismiss the effect *having* money had on some people. Sometimes more than enough was never enough. Poverty and desperation bred crime. But so did greed.

He was made to wait almost an hour this time before Mark would see him, and when he was admitted, Fairhaven showed some resentment at being questioned again.

"Sit down, Naylor. I don't have much time for you today, but then, I can't imagine what more you want from me."

"I just thought I would stop in and see if you had heard anything from our young footman, my lord," answered Gideon.

"Nothing. And I am not sure why you would expect me to," replied Mark impatiently.

"You are, after all, his employer."

"Was, Naylor, was."

"You would not take the young man back as a clerk, then, my lord?"

"Not after his desertion, no. But as I said before, Naylor, I doubt that he will even come back. He is out of the city now, or dead, I am sure of it."

"Well, well, you may be right, my lord. But I am going to put a bit more of my time into it, nevertheless."

Halesworth got up, and as he walked to the door, gave a less-than-heartfelt apology for the fact that he was going to have to see Gideon out, and wished him luck.

Gideon sauntered out of the building, very satisfied with himself. If Fairhaven were guilty, then the knowledge that Gideon was still looking for Jim should nudge him into action.

Indeed, Mark was very eager to finish up his business for the day and get down to the pub to meet Drabble.

Drabble was late, but explained that he hadn't wanted to leave Naylor until he seemed settled into the Garrick's Head for the evening.

"Has he found anything yet?"

"Not that Oi can see, m'lord. 'E's visited two 'ouses in Mayfair."

"Whose?"

"Oi was able to discover that one was Lord Ashford's and the other Lord Barrand's."

"I suppose that makes sense," said Mark after a moment. "He would be questioning Ashford further and reporting to Lord Barrand. No forays into any other parts of the city?"

"Only to a bawdy 'ouse that night, m'lord," said Drabble with a leer, a wink, and a sniffle.

"Did he appear to be on business or, ah, pleasure?"

"Oh, Oi would say pleasure, m'lord, from the time 'e was in there. "Or else 'e were doing some werry intense questioning, hif you know wot Oi mean." Drabble drew his sleeve across his nose and Mark looked at him in distaste.

"And he doesn't suspect he is being followed?"

" 'E 'asn't twigged me, m'lord. Nor will 'e. Oi told you Oi was good."

"So you did. Well, back to the Garrick's Head, and we'll meet tomorrow night at the same time."

Gideon was in the same corner with his actor friends when Drabble slipped back in and took a place at the bar. Gideon got up to leave a little earlier than the night before, and was almost to the door before Drabble realized he was leaving. He hoped he wouldn't attract any attention from the barkeep as he slopped his almost-full tankard down and left before getting his change.

He was just in time to see Gideon heading off in the same direction as before and assumed he was going back for another night of whoring. But Gideon passed Mrs. Doyle's and kept going. It was ten minutes later that he stopped across the street from an obviously better class of house and stood for a few minutes, as though trying to decide whether to go in or not.

Drabble watched from the shadows. While Gideon was standing there, the door opened and a customer was shown out by a very authentic-looking footman. Drabble didn't make the connection immediately. It was only when Gideon stepped across the street and spoke to the young man that it clicked. Footman. Young. Could it be this Jim? Could Naylor have found him and was he keeping him hidden for some reason? Drabble was tired and tempted to go home. But what if he weren't Jim? Lord Fairhaven wouldn't hire him again. And he could be wrong. Maybe he needed to do a little more research. Maybe, he thought, fingering his money, an hour or two in bed with one of the girls could be considered part of his job.

He waited fifteen minutes and then went up to the door and knocked.

* * *

Gideon had planned to get Jim into Mrs. Spencer's parlor and question him first, then decide what to do about the rest of the evening. But Mrs. Spencer was coming out of the parlor just as he got in the front door. This evening she was dressed in purple silk that clung very satisfactorily, and she acknowledged Gideon with a smile.

"Have you decided to shift your loyalties, then, Mr. Naylor? Or is this visit business, not pleasure?"

"A little bit of both, I hope, Mrs. Spencer. May I speak with you privately?"

She hesitated and then said: "Of course. Jim," she called, "send any customer to Carrie to sort out."

"Yes, madam."

Gideon followed her into the parlor and waited for her to sit down. She didn't.

"What can I do to help you, Mr. Naylor? Answer more questions about Jim? Or tell you about my young ladies?"

Surely Mrs. Blisse Spencer's face was a most intriguing one, thought Gideon. Once again, her smile barely widened her eyes, but her mouth—ah, that mouth! He should be questioning her and Jim, he knew, but he couldn't ignore the lushness of her lips.

"Actually, I have a question or two for you, Mrs. Spencer, but perhaps that can wait."

"Ah, so you are interested in one of my young women. Do you like them innocent or experienced, Mr. Naylor?"

"Oh, experienced, Mrs. Spencer. I am not one who is attracted by enacted virginity, nor do I approve of the practice of deflowering young girls just in from the country," he added, trying not to sound too hard. It was easier to do that, he thought to himself with a grin, than to keep another part of himself soft in her presence.

"Nor do I, Mr. Naylor. Some of my girls are young, but they are the ones who have come to me from the streets and from abusive employers or customers. I am not one of those who serves up children, I assure you. But now that we have established that you like some experience in a woman," she said with a practiced smile, "tell me if you prefer blondes or brunettes."

"Brunettes, most definitely. In fact," said Gideon, looking at Mrs. Spencer's black hair, "I most appreciate the darkest hues. Although it is rare to see a natural raven-haired beauty."

Mrs. Spencer looked at him shrewdly. "Well, I am afraid I have no black-haired women here, Mr. Naylor. But I do have a very lovely nut-brown maid."

"But the more I think about it, the more I realize how my heart is set on black," Gideon replied, gazing innocently at Mrs. Spencer's hair.

"I see. I am afraid I am the only black-haired woman in the house, Mr. Naylor, and I am no longer available to customers."

Gideon moved closer. They really were almost of a height, he thought ruefully, and their eyes were almost level.

"That is a great disappointment, Mrs. Spencer," he said, reaching out and lightly touching a wisp of hair that had worked free of her Psyche knot.

"Is it."

"Indeed, yes." Gideon let his hand follow the hair down the line of her jaw until his fingers were near her mouth. He let his little finger gently trace the curves of her upper lip and Mrs. Spencer let out a small sigh.

Damn the man, she thought, he drew her right in, just as he had drawn Jim. He didn't force, this Gideon Naylor, he just let the stillness he created do the trick. She hadn't been with a customer for over five years. Unfortunately, that meant she hadn't been with a man for that long either. Not that she had missed it. Not that she had ever enjoyed it, except for the years that she had been with her protector.

"I don't suppose that I could convince you to relax your policy for one night," whispered Gideon, his finger lingering on her lips.

"I might consider giving you an hour, Mr. Naylor," she whispered back.

Gideon lowered his face and gave her a gentle kiss on the mouth. "Good."

31

As they left the parlor, Mrs. Spencer told Jim that Carrie was in charge for the next hour or so and led Gideon up the stairs to the room she had once given to Jim. She turned away from him and started to undress matter-of-factly, but Gideon placed his hands on her shoulders and turned her to him for another, this time, longer and deeper kiss.

"No need to be so businesslike," he whispered.

"But it is business, Mr. Naylor."

"It is good business to please the customer, Mrs. Spencer. And it pleases me to please you."

"A novel concept in a whorehouse," she said, with a low, shaky laugh.

Gideon's fingers were gently untying the tapes of her gown, and the cool and self-possessed Mrs. Spencer shivered as he brushed her neck and spine.

He let her dress fall to her waist and gently cupped one breast, his thumb circling her nipple as he kissed her once again.

This time she responded naturally and hungrily, and as they stood there kissing, Gideon undid the rest of her gown and let it fall to the floor. Mrs. Spencer wore no underslip, and Gideon reveled in the soft flesh that pressed against him. She lowered her hand to his trousers, but he forestalled her, turning her until he had her back to the bed, and then lowering her onto the coverlet.

Gideon did not turn away as he undressed, and Blisse lay there watching as he slowly undid his trousers. His manhood sprang free. He stood there, a very satisfying figure of a man despite his lack of inches and receding hairline. He lay down beside her and, leaning on his elbow, ran his fingers up her thighs and then between them, letting the caressing fingers brush the triangular thatch of hair, which was light brown, not black. Gideon smiled at her.

"Just as I guessed. Your hair is a little too black to be natural, Mrs. Spencer."

"At least it is still abundant, Mr. Naylor," she replied, her fingers tracing his hairline.

"*Touché*, Mrs. Spencer."

"My name is Blisse."

"And mine Gideon," he answered, stroking her with his fingers until she lifted her hips to meet him.

Her hand reached down to him and he said: "No, you have spent enough years pleasuring men," and he knelt on top of her, moving himself up and down where his fingers had been, until she was moaning beneath him. Only then did he slip inside her, stroking her gently at first and then forcefully, holding himself back while he reached down and added his subtle fingering to the music he was making on her body. It was only after she climaxed in a series of shuddering gasps that he let himself experience his own release.

They lay locked in each other's arms for a while, neither wanting to break their closeness with words. Finally Gideon gently stroked her hair back from her face and said: "You are very appropriately named, my dear."

"Ah, yes," she replied bitterly, turning away from him. "That is what the first man said."

"And who was he?"

"Our vicar. Yes, he said it was like experiencing the bliss of paradise. For him, you understand," she added ironically.

"Gideon continued stroking her hair. "How old were you?"

"Fourteen."

"Did you not tell anyone?"

"Who would have believed me? No, our vicar was the

younger son of a viscount, happily married with three children, and I was the local shopkeeper's daughter. His wife caught us. I was locked in my room with no food for three days. When I wouldn't 'confess' my sins, my father beat me and threw me out. I came to London and you can guess the rest. It is not a very original story."

Gideon leaned down and kissed her neck. "No, I have heard variations of it from the likes of Annie and Grace. How did you come to own your own house?"

"I was lucky to have been taken into a high-class house when I was in my twenties. I met a man—a gentleman. Another younger son. He became my protector for four years. When he finally married, he gave me a parting gift so that I could set up on my own."

"You loved him?"

"I loved him, the more fool I."

"I don't think it foolish," said Gideon.

Blisse started to sit up. "I believe our time is up, Mr. Naylor."

"Gideon. Must you leave?"

"I'm a good businesswoman, Mr. Naylor."

"Gideon."

"*Gideon.* I must get back downstairs."

"But Carrie seems like such a competent girl," he said with a grin, grasping her wrist gently. "And I am, after all, a paying customer. Surely it is good business to ensure that I, er, come again. I am beginning to like it here very much. I will miss Grace and Annie—"

"I have a girl who would make you forget them, Gideon. She is young and fresh. I will make sure you get Nancy when you return."

"But as I told you, I prefer experience."

"Well, then, Carrie would be just the thing," said Blisse, trying to stand up, but Gideon would not release her.

"No," continued Gideon, in his mildest tones, "I prefer older women." He pulled himself up so that he was sitting behind her, his legs on either side of hers. He let go of her wrist and his hand sought her out again. She arched her back against him and he nuzzled her neck while he brought her to an excruciatingly slow and pleasurable climax. She relaxed against him for a moment and then, pushing him back on the bed, took her hand and stroked him rhythmically until he thought he would burst. And just before he did, she lowered herself down on him so that he climaxed in seconds inside her sweet, warm darkness.

They slept in each other's arms, and when Gideon awoke, he lay there, looking down at her. Her black hair was down around her shoulders and her face was, for the first time since he'd met her, at one with her mouth: relaxed and tender. Gideon had never had a woman he hadn't paid for and never a woman he had loved, for Mary had let him do no more than kiss her. Grace and Annie were sweet, they genuinely liked him, but ultimately—they were all business. No money, no time with them.

Blisse Spencer was all business too, so why had this felt different? He looked over at his coat, lying crumpled on the floor. He should slip out of bed, put his money on the table, and be gone. And if he were smart, never come back, no matter what he had told her.

But he didn't want to pay for this. He wanted to pretend it had been real desire between them, not just the usual transaction between whore and customer.

Blisse stirred in his arms and opened her eyes. For a moment or two they were unfocused, and as innocent as he expected they'd been at fourteen. Then, as she remembered where she was, they grew hard. But before she could say anything, Gideon spoke.

"I know. It is late. You are a busy woman. But I have a proposition for you."

She looked puzzled.

"I find that I wish to pretend that this afternoon was real . . . that is . . . that we were only a man and a woman who desired each other. I do not want to pay you."

Her eyes opened wide. "Now, before you become angry, hear me out. I will come back some other time and pay you double for Carrie or Nancy or whomever you choose. Will that be satisfactory?"

"How do I know you will come back, Mr. Naylor?"

"I can only give you my word."

"Very well," she replied, with no expression in her voice. "I will trust you."

"Thank you, Mrs. Spencer. And now I must be going." Gideon got up and dressed quickly, looking back only once. Mrs. Spencer lay there, looking up at him with those hard eyes of hers. He must have been a fool to think there had been anything different about this coupling. He must have sounded a right fool just then, telling her his feelings. He tucked in his shirt, thrust his arms into his coat, and muttering good-bye, was gone.

Blisse Spencer lay there. Her eyes had softened remarkably as soon as Gideon shut the door. Could he truly have felt what she had? A coming to life of what she thought was dead forever? Of course not. She was being ridiculous. She was an aging whore. She was good. She'd never denied that. She'd convinced men more times than she could count that her desire was real. Obviously she hadn't lost her expertise, for she'd just done it again. He'd realize that and not return. Or come back asking for Carrie or Nancy. Not Blisse Spencer with her dyed black hair and foolish heart.

While Gideon had been with Mrs. Spencer, Drabble had bought himself time with Lizzie, one of the more experienced girls. Carrie had been about to give him Nancy, but Jim shook his head behind Drabble and she shrugged her shoulders and called Lizzie down. As Drabble went up the stairs behind her, he heard Carrie say, "Now Jim, I know you like Nancy, but you can't be holding her back like that."

Hit's Fair'aven's footman, thought Drabble as he sniffed after Lizzie's shapely bottom. *Well, now, Oi can enjoy myself tonight and inform Lord Fair'aven in the morning.*

"He was not," Lizzie announced to Carrie and Jim and Gideon later, as Jim and the girl stood in the hallway seeing the Runner out, "the most repulsive customer I've had. But that dripping and dropping great nose of his—and the snuffling! It was hard not to laugh, especially since he snuffled through the, er . . . crucial moment, if you know what I mean."

They all laughed and Gideon bade them good night and set off for home. He had never gotten to question Jim, he thought, but then, that gave him an excuse to come back very soon.

It wasn't until he had gone a few blocks that the memory stirred. The snuffling man in the Garrick's Head. A snuffling man here at Mrs. Spencer's. But surely there were plenty of dripping noses all over London. But what if someone had been following him the other night? What if Lord Fairhaven had hired a man so that if Gideon got to Jim, Fairhaven did too? Damn. If what he suspected were so, then Fairhaven would have the information in the morning. It looked as if he, Gideon, would have to do some following himself. And that meant no sleep tonight.

32

Gideon took up his watch across from Fairhaven's. It was hard to stay awake, for he was not only tired, but relaxed. It was hard to keep his mind on the street and not get lost in recollections of his time with Blisse. Just before dawn, he dozed off for a short while, but luckily the early-morning clatter awakened him. He watched as the vendors filled the street, but saw no one else. He was wondering if his intuition had proved wrong when he heard and saw Drabble coming down the street. The man looked very sure of himself when he knocked on the door and was admitted by the butler.

He came out slightly subdued, and Gideon guessed that Mark Halesworth wanted no more connection between himself and his spy. Well, now, Mr. Snuffle was going to be followed. Followed and grabbed.

Gideon gave him fifteen minutes, so that they were out of sight of any spectators, and then, pushing by Drabble, stopped suddenly and pushed him back into an alley.

"Wot do you think you are doing?" whined Drabble. "Oi've committed no crime."

"You're lying. I am sure that Lord Fairhaven paid you a pretty penny for following an officer of the law and for the information you just gave him."

Drabble tried to bluff. "Wot information? Lord Fair'aven give the loikes of me money? Walker!"

Holding Drabble against the wall by his throat, Gideon rummaged through his pockets and found a guinea. "A guinea per week, eh? Just like a Runner. Now why don't you tell me exactly what Lord Fairhaven paid you for? Or I'll see you in Newgate for interfering with the king's justice."

Drabble didn't hesitate. Fear seemed to dry him up, for with only one or two sniffs, he got out the whole story.

"And what does Fairhaven plan to do?" asked Gideon when Drabble had finished.

" 'E asked me to meet 'im at the Golden Crown tonight so Oi could take 'im to Mrs. Spencer's. 'E'll see wot this Jim knows . . ."

"And then?"

"Oi don't know. Hit all depends on the boy. Hif 'e saw somefing, well then . . . Oi don't think Lord Fair'aven will be too pleased with 'im, will 'e?"

"Let me tell you what you are going to do, Mr.—"

"Drabble."

"Mr. Drabble. You are going to do just what Fairhaven asked. And you are not going to tell him about this little conversation, are you?"

"No, sir. Of course not."

"Good. I don't know what Jim saw, by the way. He may not have seen anything. But I do wonder what Fairhaven thinks there was for him to see."

"Oi don't know, guv. Oi am sure Oi don't, and 'is lordship didn't tell me."

Gideon shook Drabble hard enough so that his head bounced rhythmically against the wall. "You will do as I say, won't you, Drabble?"

"Yes, sir. Oi don't want no trouble with the Runners, Mr. Naylor."

"Good. Now off with you."

Drabble tried for a little dignity as Gideon let him go. He straightened his collar and coat, but after one look at Gideon's face, he scurried away down the street, as Gideon watched with grim amusement. "Well, Lord Ashford will be happy to hear about this development in the case," he muttered to himself.

Indeed, Tony was thrilled when he heard of Gideon's progress.

"Don't give me too much credit, my lord," said Gideon. "I can't believe he followed me for so long without my noticing. If he hadn't given in to a certain appetite . . ." Gideon was very disappointed in himself.

"But you put two and two together, Naylor," protested Tony.

"Yes. A sniffle here, a snuffle there," he said sarcastically.

"You found Jim, and now you'll find the connection to Fairhaven. All we have to do now is get Mark to confess."

Gideon heard the "we." "I am calling in another Runner, my lord."

"Oh, no, you're not. We both think Mark Halesworth killed Claudia and let me rot in Newgate for it. Would have let me hang. I am going to take part in this," said Tony, with a look in his eyes that his subalterns would have recognized.

"We don't know for sure that Mark Halesworth killed Lady Fairhaven."

"Do you have any serious doubts, Naylor?"

"Not a one, my lord. You are welcome to accompany me. I wish to be there by early evening so that we don't miss him. I will be back to pick you up at five."

"I'll be ready."

When they arrived at Mrs. Spencer's, Carrie opened the door and Gideon had a moment of panic. Maybe Jim had run again, or maybe Fairhaven had gotten here ahead of him. But when he inquired, Carrie only smiled and winked and said that Jim was spending a little time with Nancy.

"Is Mrs. Spencer around?" Gideon asked.

"She usually takes a rest in the afternoon, Mr. Naylor, since she is up most of the night."

"Of course. We will wait in the parlor, Carrie. Send Jim in as soon as he comes down. And Carrie . . ."

"Yes, Mr. Naylor?"

"You remember Lizzie's customer, Mr. Drabble?"

"The great snuffler?"

"That's the one. He will be back tonight. Don't admit him before you have told me."

"Yes, sir. Er, does your friend here want to wait with you, or is he in the mood for some company?" Carrie batted her eyelashes at Tony and pulled at her dress as though to smooth it, although her real purpose was to make sure that more of her bosom was revealed.

Tony gave her a quick grin. "Not tonight, luv, I am sorry."

"There is no harm in trying, sir," she said as she whisked out.

Tony gazed around the parlor. "For the neighborhood, this seems a decent house, Naylor."

"Yes, and when Jim is on, that only adds to the atmosphere."

Tony smiled. "I can imagine. Of course, I don't frequent these places myself. I've spent all my time at Seventy-five St. James Street since I've been home. And on the Peninsula there were plenty of willing women." Tony was silent for a moment and then asked: "Are you married, Naylor?"

Gideon looked over at him in surprise. "No, my lord. A Runner's life is hardly one a woman would want to share. Out all hours. Consorting with thieves and worse. No, I wouldn't ask a woman to put up with that."

"It must be a lonely life. Rather like a soldier's."

"About the same, my lord. Although when I was in the Forty-seventh Foot I thought I had someone to come home to. But she got tired of waiting."

"After this is all over, I suppose I will be settling into a rather monkish life myself, Naylor. Up early in the morning, riding the estate and early to bed. A life of virtuous maturity," Tony added with a whimsical smile. "Not how I ever pictured myself. But I suppose we all have to grow up."

Gideon was too curious not to ask. "What of Lady Joanna, my lord? She is a good friend and still unattached."

"She is most definitely not waiting for me, I can assure you. She just hasn't found her match yet. And Joanna deserves someone . . . someone less like me and more like Ned," Tony finished slowly.

"She was certainly very concerned about you, my lord." Gideon felt he had gone far enough. There was only so much he could say without seeming to pry into what was the private affair of an earl, no matter how accessible that earl was.

"We have cared for each other a long time, Naylor, but only as friends."

Gideon was about to risk one more hint, but the parlor door opened and Jim walked in.

Tony stood up and Jim looked at him, dumbfounded.

"Lord Ashford!"

"Yes, Jim. Come to thank you for your statement, as far as it went," Gideon commented dryly.

"Now, Naylor, I *am* grateful to Jim."

"It was the least I could do," Jim answered, looking down at the floor.

"And what would be the most, Jim?" Gideon asked. "Telling us that Lord Fairhaven was the last person to see Lady Fairhaven alive? Or perhaps that you saw the murder itself?"

Jim's face became set and white, but he said nothing.

"Come now, Jim, I know it all. Or almost all," said Gideon. "Far better you tell me now. I suspect we don't have too much time before Lord Fairhaven gets here."

Jim looked ready to bolt. "How did he find me?"

Gideon sighed. "Unfortunately, through me, I hate to confess. Drabble—you remember Mr. Drabble?" said Gideon with an exaggerated sniff. "He was hired by Fairhaven to follow me."

Jim's shoulders slumped. He looked over at Tony apologetically. "Shortly after you left, my lord, Lord Fairhaven arrived and I admitted him to the library. Dawson had asked me to stay up so that I could see her ladyship to bed. I was getting tired, and I thought if I looked in to see if she needed anything, she might take pity on me and send me up too." Jim stopped.

"Go on," Gideon said softly.

"Lord Fairhaven had his hands around her neck and I saw her collapse. I panicked and ran. I don't think he saw me, but I didn't wait to find out. I didn't know you had been charged, honestly, my lord," he said to Tony.

"No hard feelings, Jim. I probably would have done the same thing."

"I couldn't tell you the other day, Mr. Naylor. I was too scared that if I came forward as a witness, Lord Fairhaven would somehow find a way to keep me quiet."

"I would have pushed you harder, lad, had I needed to."

"What do we do now, Naylor?"

"I think we'll let Jim answer the door. He's not going to kill you on the doorstep, Jim," he added with a grim smile, seeing the look of fear on Jim's face. "You'll show him into the parlor and we'll wait down the hall."

"But I'll be alone with him."

"Remember, he doesn't yet know that you saw him. If you feel you are in immediate danger, just—" Gideon looked around the room. "Just knock over that vase. We'll be listening for it and come right in. Can you do it?"

Jim took a deep breath. "I think so, sir. I owe it to Lady Fairhaven. She was always very kind to me."

33

It was only half an hour before Jim opened the door to Drabble and Lord Fairhaven, but it had felt like eons. He was almost relieved to see his former employer give him a patently false smile and telling him he was delighted to have found him.

"Come in, my lord. I will find Mrs. Spencer, who can take care of whatever you need."

"No, no, Jim, what I need is to speak with you," said Fairhaven. "Is there someplace we can be private?"

"Yes, my lord. We can use the parlor."

"Drabble, keep watch at the door, will you?"

"Yes, my lord."

Fairhaven walked ahead of Jim and opened the parlor door himself. "After you, Jim," he said. He closed the door behind them. "Sit down, lad, sit down," he added.

Jim sat, and Mark stood over him. "You left Lady Fairhaven's very suddenly, Jim."

"Yes, my lord," Jim answered, trying to sound matter-of-fact about it.

"Would you care to tell me why?"

"Well, my lord, you see, Lord Ashford had told me of their betrothal on his way out and I thought that after I gave you that piece of information, my job was over anyway."

"But you never *did* come to tell me that, did you, Jim?"

"Er, no, my lord. I was planning to that next morning, but then, when I heard about Lady Fairhaven's murder, it didn't seem to make any difference anyway."

"But why didn't you just come back to your job at the

warehouse?" Mark's voice was calm and reasonable, but Jim felt as if he were being stalked, very slowly and carefully, by a tiger.

"I found I enjoyed my short time as a footman, my lord. It must be in the blood," he added, with a nervous little laugh.

"So you sought out a job as footman in a bawdy house? Does your family have a history of that sort of employment, Jim?" Fairhaven asked sarcastically.

"It seemed a beginning, my lord."

"I would have thought a reference from me would have given you a better start, Jim."

"Uh, yes, but I didn't want to trouble you in the middle of your family tragedy, my lord." Jim had had some time to think of a vaguely plausible story, but the more he said, the more ridiculous it seemed. But what else was he to say?

Mark leaned forward and put his hands on the arms of Jim's chair, effectively trapping him.

"I don't think I believe you, Jim."

"I swear it is the truth, my lord."

Mark continued as though he had not heard. "I think you saw something that night and were terrified and ran for cover. *I* think you may even have seen Lady Fairhaven's killer."

What the hell am I to do now? thought Jim. *I can't knock over the vase. I can't even get out of the chair. And he hasn't confessed anything. He has to admit to it in someone's hearing so if anything happens to me, he won't get away with it.*

He took a deep breath and let it out as though he were expressing great relief. "You have guessed, my lord. I did see the murderer, and I ran because I was terrified he might have seen me."

"Did you recognize him, Jim?"

Jim hesitated, and tried to look both fearful and sly at the same time. "I think I may have, but I am not really sure. My parents have not much to live on, you know, my lord," he added.

"And what do your parents have to do with it?"

"I was thinking that if I *did* recognize the murderer, he might want to give them a pension to keep me quiet."

"And if he did that, what would you do, Jim?"

"I have heard that there are many opportunities in America for young men who are willing to work hard, your lordship."

"But how would you get word to the murderer, Jim?"

"I rather think I am speaking with him now, my lord."

Fairhaven lifted one hand from the chair arm and reached out to run his thumb along Jim's neck. "Why should I pay for something when I could so easily . . ."

"I am afraid you have chosen the wrong sort of house, sir," said a voice at the door.

Jim and Fairhaven had been so intent that neither had heard the door open. Blisse Spencer closed it behind her. "If you want a young man, you will have to go someplace else."

Fairhaven straightened up and Jim sank back in the chair.

"Jim, I think you had better get back to your post," said Mrs. Spencer.

Jim wasn't sure what to do. He couldn't leave Mrs. Spencer alone with a murderer. On the other hand, if he got out, he could get Gideon. . . .

"Go ahead, Jim," said Fairhaven. "Perhaps I was mistaken. I thought we had the same thing in mind."

"I think we do, my lord, only not here," said Jim, closing the door as he left and looking desperately down the hall for Naylor and Lord Ashford.

Blisse Spencer looked puzzled. Jim's interest in Nancy had been very obvious and sweet. Whatever did he mean? She turned to Fairhaven and said, "I can give you the address of an appropriate house, if you wish, sir."

"Thank you, Mrs. Spencer."

"Let me show you out."

They were almost to the parlor door when it flew open. Without a second's hesitation, Fairhaven pulled Mrs. Spencer in front of him and backed away from Gideon Naylor.

"Drabble!" he shouted.

Tony Varden pulled Drabble into the doorway. "I am afraid he is otherwise occupied, Lord Fairhaven."

Gideon had a pistol in his hand and took careful aim at Fairhaven.

"I wouldn't, if I were you, Naylor, or I'll kill the woman," said Mark, who had his hands at the base of Blisse Spencer's neck.

Gideon looked into Blisse's face and said in a cold, hard voice: "Do what you want, Fairhaven. Why should I care what happens to an old whore?"

Blisse would not give Gideon the satisfaction of revealing how much he had hurt her with those words. So she was expendable, was she? She had guessed by now that it was Lord Fairhaven who held her. The man Jim was running from. The same Fairhaven who had killed Lady Fairhaven by pressing against her arteries. She could feel Fairhaven's thumbs moving slowly and inexorably to the pulse points. But if he did it, he was dead anyway, she thought. Wasn't it to his advantage to use her as a shield?

"I am warning you, Naylor. I have no reason not to kill her."

"And I repeat: Do what you want, my lord. We will have you for two murders then."

Blisse knew there was only one thing to do: go down before Fairhaven's hands or Gideon's pistol made her do so. She slumped suddenly in Fairhaven's arms and in the split second that Fairhaven looked down in surprise, Gideon was next to him, pistol cocked and resting against Fairhaven's forehead.

"Let her down gently, my lord."

Blisse let herself slide down to the floor and lay there as dazed as if she were indeed unconscious.

"Jim!"

"Yes, sir."

"Get me some rope."

"Yes, sir."

Jim was back in a moment, and in a short time both Drabble and Fairhaven were immobilized.

"My God," said Tony, leaning over Blisse, "you are indeed terrible with the terrible. I hope he hasn't killed her."

"He hadn't enough time, my lord," replied Gideon. "I knew I could get there as soon as she lost consciousness."

"I hope she has only fainted," said Tony.

Blisse decided she could open her eyes. She pushed herself up, surprised at how weak she felt. "He didn't even get that far, my lord," she said. "I only pretended to faint. I decided it was up to me to save myself," she added, her eyes hard and her mouth trembling.

"Good for you, Mrs. Spencer," said Jim.

"And good for you, Jim," Tony said. "You must have been terrified."

"A little," Jim admitted. "Especially when Mrs. Spencer walked in on us."

"Get us a cab, Jim," said Naylor, who hadn't even looked over in Mrs. Spencer's direction. "We've got to get these two down to Bow Street."

Tony lifted Blisse to her feet. "Do you have anything to drink, Mrs. Spencer?" he asked, and she pointed out a decanter of brandy sitting on a side table. He sat her down on the sofa and poured her a glass and one for himself.

"Do you want one, Naylor?"

"No, my lord, not when I am on a job."

The heat of the brandy stopped Blisse's trembling and she looked over at Gideon. He stood next to Fairhaven, pistol still cocked, his face unreadable. He was a very different Gideon from the one who had drawn Jim out. Who had brought her to the bedroom for the first time in five years. This Gideon left no space at all for approach. It wasn't just his pistol that put him in charge of the whole room. It was an energy that was almost palpable. Some women would be attracted to that energy, she thought. Not she. She preferred a man who let you in, like the Gideon who had taken her to bed. Well, she would never see either Gideon again, thank God. And next time, she'd know better than to let down her guard.

34

By the early afternoon of the next day, the news was out: Mark Halesworth, Lord Fairhaven, had been arrested for the murder of his cousin, and Tony Varden was completely vindicated. As always, there were those amongst the gossips who claimed to have had their doubts all along. "Mark Halesworth was a cold man, as I always said," or "Despite his gambling, Tony Varden never did seem the type to murder anyone," went these refrains.

For Joanna and Tony, the denouement was almost anticlimactic. They were both dazed by the sudden change in attitude. Joanna was ecstatic, she told herself, that her faith in Tony had been justified. But if that were so, then why did she feel so empty? Perhaps it was because she had had a purpose for the last few weeks, that purpose demonstrating her faith in Tony. Was she so perverse that she would prefer Tony in jeopardy so that she could stand by him? Had she hoped, at some level, that the crisis would bring them together?

She wore one of her most beautiful new dresses that night. Her card was almost full by the time Tony arrived and she could only offer him a country dance. He was surrounded by well-wishers. Those who had been avoiding him for weeks were now rushing up to offer their congratulations.

The hypocrisy of the *ton* never ceased to amaze Joanna. Women who would not have let their daughters dance with him a few days ago were dragging them over for an introduction. Not that his popularity would last, thought Joanna cynically. The notoriety would fade in a week or so and then these same mothers would remember that he was only a bankrupt earl.

Tony himself was surprised that his reception didn't make him feel any better. He spent the evening with a smile pasted on his face and a stock of platitudes on his lips, which he trotted out as people congratulated him. No one seemed to be thinking of Claudia, only the scandal of Lord Fairhaven's arrest. He missed Claudia, and at the same time realized, with some surprise, that if she had been miraculously restored to life, he would have ended their engagement, Ashford or no Ashford. But he would have liked to have talked to her as a friend and share his confusion with someone. Claudia would have understood that the events of the past few weeks had changed him profoundly. Although a part of him wanted to bolt for St. James Street, he knew that he neither could nor would gamble again. He also knew that it was time to return home and begin to learn Ned's strategies for setting things to rights. And Claudia was also the only person, besides Ned, that he could imagine confiding in regarding his new and disturbing feelings for Joanna.

Tony was even more in need of Claudia the next day when he was summoned to the reading of her will. It took place in the Fairhaven library, with the late Lord Fairhaven looking over the shoulder of the family solicitor as though to say: "Foolish woman, but I always loved her for her warm heart and generous spirit. And now that she is with me again, you're welcome to the money, Ashford."

Tony had assumed he was there to receive some little keepsake. When he discovered he was to inherit a substantial amount of money, he sat there dazed by the news. "Thank you, my dear friend," he whispered. He could almost hear her answer: "I always had great faith in you, Tony." *I will not disappoint you, Claudia,* he silently pledged.

As he walked home it slowly dawned on him that he was now free. Ashford would be safe. He could hire a competent estate manager if he wanted to and buy back his commission. He could return to the excitement of life in the military, and let his mother run the household.

The realization did not make him feel the way he would have at the beginning of the Season. Something had shifted in him during his ordeal. Oh, he would never be Ned. But neither could he ever be again the same devil-may-care Tony Varden. He was terrified by the thought of the responsibilities he had inherited. But underneath the familiar terror was a small spark of excitement. It was a sort of gamble, he thought with a smile. A private wager. Himself against the world's opinion of him and his own past.

Without realizing it, he had turned into Berkeley Square and was in front of the Barrand house. His pace quickened as he bounded up the front steps, so eager was he to tell Joanna his news.

"Lady Joanna is dressing for her morning ride," the butler informed him. "If you will wait in the morning room, perhaps she can see you for a few minutes, my lord."

Tony was pacing back and forth when Joanna entered, looking very attractive in her new hunter's green riding habit.

"You are looking very pretty this morning, Joanna."

"Thank you, Tony. And you are looking in alt about something. I only have a few minutes, for Lord Oakford and his sister will be here shortly."

Tony frowned. Lord Oakford was a widower who had seemingly discovered Joanna during the last few weeks. He had become very attentive and Tony wondered exactly what Joanna's feelings were towards him.

"I have received some rather amazing news, Jo. Claudia left me a great deal of money. I haven't quite grasped it in yet, but it seems as if I have received a last-minute reprieve and Ashford is saved."

Joanna impulsively put out her hands and grasped Tony's. "I am so happy for you, Tony. She must have loved you very much."

Tony's hands shook and when Joanna looked up into his

face, she was surprised to see it wet with tears. Tony let go and stood up suddenly, turning his back, and trying to dry his eyes quickly.

And you must have loved her more than you knew, thought Joanna, suddenly very tired.

Tony cleared his throat. "It is her faith that touches me more than her affection. I knew I had her heart, but at the end I was afraid I might have killed her trust in me." He turned and gave Joanna a tentative smile. "Of course, there was a good reason for that. Anyway, I wanted you to be the first to hear, Jo, before the *ton* got hold of it."

"Thank God, Mark Halesworth was arrested."

"My God, I hadn't even thought of that! If the will had been read earlier, I'd be back in Newgate!"

"I think Gideon Naylor had something to say in the matter," Joanna told him.

"Naylor?"

"Yes, he had received hints from Fairhaven and checked with the family lawyers about the will. He asked them to hold off until he got further in his investigations."

"He wouldn't have done that had you not convinced him that I was innocent, Jo. Another woman whose faith and trust I didn't deserve," he said in an almost inaudible voice.

Joanna wanted none of his gratitude. "Well, what will you do, Tony?" she asked briskly to change the mood of the conversation. "Hire a manager and go back to your regiment?"

"You know me so well, don't you, Jo?"

Joanna's heart sank. She had so hoped that this spring had changed him.

"It was my first thought," he admitted. He was fingering a celadon vase on the mantelpiece. The green glaze made him think of the flecks of green in Jo's eyes. He wanted to look more closely to see if it was indeed the same green. To see himself in her eyes. What would they reflect? Only the image of an old friend? Or someone new and different? He didn't have the courage to risk it. "But all of this seems to have changed me," he continued. He smiled his most charming smile and ran his hands through his hair. "Oh, I'll never be like Ned or my father. But I mean to take up my responsibilities as earl as best I can. It will be nice to be neighbors again, Jo," he told her softly.

Someone knocked at the door and Joanna said quickly, "That must be Lord Oakford. I don't want to keep him waiting, Tony. I am happy that you will be back at Ashford full time. Perhaps we can ride together again." She was almost to the door when she added over her shoulder, "In the fall. I will be visiting my godmother in Cumbria for much of the summer."

Well, that was that. Thank God he hadn't made an utter fool of himself, gazing into her eyes like some mooncalf boy. Without thinking, he hurled the celadon vase into the fireplace. It made a very satisfactory crash, which brought a footman into the morning room.

"The vase slipped through my fingers, William. Please tell Lady Barrand I will replace it for her." The footman nodded and then winced as Tony ground a long piece of porcelain into the carpet on his way out.

When Tony got home, he instructed his man to pack. "We are going home, John. I am not facing one more rout or theater party, especially after this morning."

"Yes, my lord."

"I will be out all day and part of the evening. We will leave first thing tomorrow."

"Yes, my lord."

Tony spent the day taking care of all the business he had in town. He visited Claudia's solicitor in the afternoon and made arrangements for his debts to be paid. "I want this allowance out of the money, Reresby, and the rest goes back into Ashford."

"The allowance is rather modest, if I may say so, my lord."

"For now, it is all I am willing to take. Perhaps in a year or so, when Ashford is in better shape, I will increase it."

"That is admirable, my lord. I am happy that Lady Fairhaven's faith in you has been justified."

Tony gave him a quizzical smile. "I am sure you are relieved as well as happy, Reresby. I don't imagine her changes made you happy."

"No, my lord," the older man admitted.

"I just wish I were able to do all this under different circumstances."

"Yes. A very cold and calculating man, Lord Fairhaven. I never liked him. And he had too many years of expecting everything to come to him."

Tony got up to leave and then sat down again. "There is one other thing, Reresby. I would like to give some sort of gift to Gideon Naylor of Bow Street and a small allowance to Jim Rooke. Without them, Mark Halesworth would never have been caught. I think Lady Fairhaven would approve."

Reresby smiled. "She would, my lord, she would."

35

Tony was determined to thank Naylor before he left and so he headed for Bow Street early that evening. When he arrived at the court, he was informed he could find Naylor at the Garrick's Head around the corner.

Gideon was at his usual table when Tony walked in and he lifted his eyebrows in surprise.

Bob looked over at the door. "Someone you know, Gideon?"

"You might say so. Anthony Varden, Lord Ashford."

"The swell you got off, eh. He must be looking for you." Bob waved Tony over. "Here's the man you're looking for, my lord."

Tony gave the actor a puzzled smile.

"Oh, we know all about you, my lord," Bob said genially. "Sit down, sit down."

"Gideon, I have come to thank you."

"No need, my lord. I only did my job."

"A little more than your job. I have just come from Lady Fairhaven's solicitor."

"So the will has been read?"

"Yes, and I know that I have you to thank that it was not read any sooner. Otherwise, I could hardly have been released on lack of motive!"

"Well, I had some doubts about the case against you, my lord. And even if I hadn't, Lady Joanna would have convinced me."

"Ah, yes, Lady Joanna, Jo, my oldest and dearest friend," said Tony with a dramatic sigh.

"You sound as if you could use a drink, my lord," said Bob, waving the barmaid over. "Just like Gideon here."

"Oh?"

"You are both blue-deviled tonight over women, I would wager."

Tony looked over at Gideon and smiled. "I'll admit to it if you will."

"Bob here is a little too free with his mouth when he's had a few ales." Gideon took a long swallow from his tankard. He was usually very careful, for a Runner couldn't afford to suffer the morning-after effects of drinking. But tonight he didn't care.

"Well, Gideon, who is she?"

Gideon turned toward Tony and gave him a look of mock despair. "Mrs. Spencer."

"Mrs. Spencer! Mrs. Spencer whom you called an old whore and almost invited Fairhaven to kill?"

"Well, what choice had I, my lord? Let him know I cared about her?"

Tony thought about it for a minute. "You're right. There wasn't anything else to do. But you were so calm and cold about it."

"As one has to be in this job, my lord."

"Yes, but that aspect of you came as a complete surprise to me, as I suspect it did to Mrs. Spencer."

"Better she sees what a Runner's life is, then," said Gideon bitterly.

"Have you been back to tell her why you did it?"

"No, and I won't go back, my lord."

"Well, I think you should, Gideon. I may call you Gideon? And you must call me Tony. We've been through too much together to stand on ceremony."

Both men, although not cast away, were in that mood of bonhomie induced by the initial stage of drunkenness.

"In fact," continued Tony, "I think we should both go tonight."

After another two drinks, both were far enough gone to decide that it was an inspired and brilliant idea.

They took a hackney to Mrs. Spencer's and were surprised to be met again by Jim.

"Why are you still here, lad?" Gideon asked. "You're safe now. You can return to a clerk's job."

"Things are all at sixes and sevens, Mr. Naylor. I am not sure what I want to do, so I decide to stay on here a week or two," Jim said with an embarrassed smile.

Tony was glad that he had set aside some money for Jim and for Gideon. Jim would have more choices with a small but steady income. And in the meantime, he certainly added a touch of class to Mrs. Spencer's establishment.

"Is Mrs. Spencer in, Jim?" Tony asked, afraid Gideon wouldn't.

"Yes, my lord. If you will go into the parlor, I will get her."

It was hard for Gideon to be back in the parlor and not see Mark Halesworth's hands around Blisse's throat. It had been a horrible few minutes that he didn't think he would ever forget.

When Mrs. Spencer entered, she was dressed in midnight-blue satin that clung to every curve. She saw Tony first and greeted him with one of her rare smiles that reached her eyes. When she noticed Gideon she ignored him.

"I am surprised to see you, Lord Ashford. Shall I ring for some brandy?"

Tony laughed and refused. "I am afraid I've had quite enough for tonight. We were surprised to see Jim still out front."

"Jim's excuse is that he is looking around for something else in his time off. I suspect that the truth is he has gotten quite fond of Nancy, one of my girls. Are you here for anything in particular, my lord?"

"Uh, no . . . that is, I hadn't thought further than a short visit to see how you have recovered from your ordeal of the other night."

"I am quite restored, my lord," said Blisse coolly. "But thank you for your concern."

"But maybe I am interested in some, er, company tonight."

Gideon shot Tony a quelling look. "I thought we couldn't stay long, Lord Ashford."

"Stay as long as you like, Gideon," said Tony with an irritating wave of his hand.

Blisse went to the door and had Jim summon Carrie. "You have met her before, my lord, and she is one of my most refined girls."

"Thank you, Mrs. Spencer. I'll see you in a few hours, Gideon."

He was gone quickly, leaving Gideon and Blisse to stare at each other. Gideon noticed that Blisse's mouth was set and was looking almost as hard as her eyes. There was no tenderness there, and he decided his case was hopeless.

"Were *you* looking for some company too, Mr. Naylor?" she asked in her most businesslike tones.

"No. Yes. But not one of the girls," he added quickly as she started for the door. "I was hoping I could have some time with you, Blisse."

"I am afraid I don't see customers, Mr. Naylor. The only time I relaxed my rule I lived to regret it."

"It was only talk I meant," protested Gideon. "Here, if that feels more comfortable for you."

"I can give you a few minutes, Mr. Naylor," she said as she sat down on the edge of the sofa.

Gideon was too nervous to sit. He moved over to the side table and lifted the Chinese vase. "Jim was supposed to drop this, you know."

Blisse turned. "Drop my Ming vase! That was a gift from my younger days."

"If he had been able to do so, we would have gotten in before you and saved you from those terrible minutes."

"It was not so terrible and I was able to cope quite well, Mr. Naylor."

"Then you are even more hardened than I am, Blisse," Gideon said, coming closer. "It was the most awful two minutes of my life."

"Surely the death of an old whore would hardly make a difference to you, Mr. Naylor," Blisse said with bitter sarcasm.

"I am sorry I had to speak of you that way. I had no choice. Had I let him know what I really felt, he could have used you as a hostage. He had to think that there was nothing he could do to stop me. And he knew that once he killed you, there would be nothing between me and him."

Mrs. Spencer's posture softened slightly, although Gideon didn't notice.

"You did what you had to do, then," she said. "And you only spoke the truth, after all. I am an old whore," she said with a rueful smile. "I accept your apology, Mr. Naylor. And now I must get back to work." She started to get up, and Gideon, who was now behind her, moved closer and placed his hands on her shoulders, gently but firmly.

"You may not forgive me, but please, at least believe me. When I told Halesworth that I didn't care what happened to you, I was lying. I do care, Blisse, very much. Now you have seen me at my worst. I can understand why a woman would not wish to be intimate with a Runner. But I wanted you to know that I think of you as a very admirable and desirable woman." Gideon took his hands off her shoulders. "Tell Lord Ashford I will be waiting across the street in the pub."

Blisse stood up and walked to the door, and Gideon felt as though his whole life was walking out of the room. And then she stopped, and looking back over her shoulder, said softly: "You don't have to wait there, Gideon. This old whore would be very pleased to have a Runner as a special . . . friend."

Gideon was next to her in a minute. "You mean that? It is a hard life, Blisse. I'll have to break promises. That is indeed the only thing I can promise you."

"My life hadn't been an easy one, Gideon. But I think we can agree to give each other a little loving, can't we?"

Gideon put his hands on either side of her face. "I thank God you are a hard woman, with the presence of mind to pretend to faint in Fairhaven's arms. I would have let him get away, luv, if it had come down to it. I want you to know that." He leaned down and covered her mouth with his, stroking her face and throat, and rejoiced in the strong pulse that was racing in response to his kiss.

36

Tony had not been with a woman since his return from the Continent. Rouge et Noir had been his passion, and he had easily avoided the lures put on by *ton* widows, and the Fashionable Impure he encountered in the hells. His hour with Carrie was a wonderful release, and freed him for a while of the guilt he still felt about Claudia and the uncertainty of his new feelings for Joanna. He was generous with his thanks and his money, and told Carrie that if he weren't leaving for the country, he would surely have returned. When Jim informed him that Gideon and Mrs. Spencer were still "occupied," he smiled and slipped out the door. Jim stepped outside with him and offered his hand very hesitantly. "I am very glad I could help you, Lord Ashford, both for your sake and Lady Fairhaven's." Tony took Jim's hand. "And I am forever indebted to you, Jim. I was going to let Reresby tell you, but I have set aside a small sum of money for you out of Lady Fairhaven's bequest to me. I know she would have approved. If you go back to your clerical world, it will supplement your salary. Enable you to marry, if you wish."

Jim was speechless for a moment and then effusive with his thanks. "I have always wanted to set up my own business," he confessed. "I only became a clerk to please my parents."

"Good luck, then, Jim. I am happy to have the chance to help you to your dream."

Tony was on his way back to Ashford before noon the next day. He didn't arrive until after midnight and went straight to bed. He slept late and was groggy and disoriented in the morning. He stubbed his toe on the nightstand and cursed John for moving it to the other side of his bed before he realized he was at Ashford and not on Clarges Street. He suspected that a part of him wanted to be back in London, getting up late after a night of gaming. The idea of taking Ned's place terrified him still. He drew on his dressing gown and stood looking out the window. He could see their old gardener out amongst the roses, clipping off the deadheads. He was being followed by one of the parlor maids, who carried a basket to collect flowers for the house. His mother had always made sure there were fresh flowers in the hallways, and she particularly loved roses. She had written him from her sister's, where she had taken refuge, and accepted his invitation to come home. He hoped it was true. He hoped she had forgiven him for haring off to London and leaving all behind. He hoped she could stand the fact that he was not Ned.

Well, at least he would be bringing Ashford back to what it once was. That should gain him some welcome from his mother, his neighbors, and his tenants. It would go a long way to make up for the fact that he wasn't his brother.

For the next few weeks, Tony was so busy that he hardly had time to worry about whether he was living up to his older brother. He interviewed very carefully for his new estate manager, having retired old Buxton. He could sense his mother's disapproval and that of the tenants when he did so, but he had decided that he had to find his own style and needed someone who could start afresh with him. The atmosphere of disapproval grew even stronger when he hired Will Farre. Farre was a veteran of the Peninsula recently invalided out after the loss of an arm. He had made his way to Ashford on the recommendation of Tony's commanding officer, and Tony hired him almost immediately. Lieutenant Farre's father had managed a larger estate in Northumberland and Farre had acted as an assistant before joining the army.

"We will both start out together, Will," said Tony, pouring two glasses of Madeira for a toast.

"I promise I won't disappoint you, my lord." The lieutenant had not really hoped for much from the interview. He had been turned down so often that he was ready to go home in defeat, when Colonel Bain had suggested Ashford. He took a few sips of wine and began to feel himself relax at last. "I never thought I'd be grateful to the French for anything," he said with a grin. "Here's to them for taking my right arm. They were not to know I am left-handed!"

Farre was only a few years older than Tony and brought new ideas as well as energy and enthusiasm. They spent hours riding about the estate together, visiting every tenant in order to find out exactly what it would take to bring Ashford back to what it had been when Tony was growing up.

Tony would come home exhausted, and after a quiet meal with his mother, would fall into bed. But he was happier than he had ever thought possible. He found that the hours with Farre, going over the newer farming methods and trying to decide what to plant in the north field, were beginning to give him as much satisfaction as planning tactics against the French. And his servants and tenants were beginning to trust him. He could feel the growing warmth in their greetings to him and realized that devotion to a common cause produced camaraderie similar to that he had found in the army.

As the summer went on and he became more accustomed to his new life, however, he realized too that while he was much happier than he had ever thought possible, he was also lonely. His mother, who had always been closer to Ned, had never completely recovered from his loss. Perhaps she never would. She had no interest in how he was running the estate and kept herself occupied inside. Losing her husband and son so close together had changed and aged her, so that after dinner together, she was usually ready to retire by the time Tony went to join her in the drawing room.

There was none but Farre to talk to about his new ideas.

Or if it was wise to consider investing a part of his income in the railways.

He missed his brother terribly. And Joanna even more, if that were possible. As close as he had grown to Farre, Tony was still the earl. They were becoming friends, but there would always be a certain distance between them.

He needed someone who cared about *him*, someone who knew of his struggles, who would appreciate just what it was he was doing. He needed his old friend. But it was more than that. He was dreaming of Joanna often, and in his dreams she was not just Jo, his childhood companion, but an attractive and sensuous woman. He would awaken morning after morning in a state of arousal from her dream touch or kiss, wanting nothing more than to drift back to sleep, where he could return her kisses and tenderly lower himself down upon her, slowly bringing them both to fulfillment.

He felt mildly ashamed, for here he was, foolishly indulging himself in a fantasy. If Joanna had had any romantic interest in him, if she saw him as any more than an old friend, she would surely have made it more obvious by now. And she most certainly wouldn't be spending the summer in Cumbria!

37

Joanna returned from Keswick in mid-August, just before the harvest. Her visit with her godmother had been just what she needed after the upheaval of the spring. She was up early and spent much of her day tramping the fells, and then fell into bed exhausted at night.

Her godmother, a calm, undemanding woman, joined her in her shorter tramps and introduced her to a few of her neighbors. There were small suppers and a few country assemblies, but for the most part, a complete and needed rest after the frantic activity of the Season. By the end of her six weeks, Joanna could smile and say to herself that she only thought of Tony once a day and was resolved to keep it that way!

She arrived back home late and went straight to bed after her long journey. But she was up early the next morning and joined her parents for breakfast.

"It is lovely to have you home, my dear," said Lady Barrand, as Joanna leaned down to kiss her mother's cheek.

Lord Barrand beamed at his daughter and complimented her on her healthy appearance.

"Don't try to flatter me, Father. I know I am as brown as a berry," said Joanna with a laugh. "I am surprised I have any skin left on my nose, it has peeled so often."

"Tony looks almost as tanned as you, dear," said her mother. "In fact, he looks almost as he did when he first returned from Spain."

Damn, Joanna said to herself. *I am here only one night and already I must be reminded of him.* But she merely nodded and gave her mother a polite murmur. "Is that so, Mother?"

But her parents were very full of Tony, it seemed.

"He has thrown himself into the running of the estate, Joanna. It is quite admirable," said her father. "He's hired a new manager, but the two of them have been working together so much they may as well be partners."

"Yes, and the tenants have all come around. They were a bit leery at first, you know, given his history. But he has certainly proved himself," declared Lady Barrand.

"It would seem his ordeal in the spring did him some good, then," replied Joanna, trying to maintain a neutral tone.

"I wouldn't be at all surprised if by the fall or at the latest in the spring, he is in London looking for a wife. What do you think, my dear," said Lord Barrand, turning to his wife.

"I am certain he will assume all the responsibilities of the earldom, Thomas."

Joanna had a hard time keeping a look of mild interest on her face. But if she was only to think of Tony once a day, then this would be it, with a vengeance! She finished her breakfast quickly, and assuring her parents she was recovered from her journey, went upstairs to dress for a morning ride.

"Do you think that you overdid it a bit, Thomas?" Lady Barrand asked after Joanna left.

"Not at all. *Someone* has to bring them to their senses. And now that Tony has reformed, what could be better than to unite the two estates?"

"I am sure of Joanna's feeling, no matter how she tries to hide them. But what of Tony?"

"What *of* Tony? They are good friends. He was going to marry Claudia on the basis of friendship. Why not Joanna?"

"But Joanna might want more, dear."

"Friendship is as good a basis for marriage as any," insisted her husband.

As Joanna rode, she tried to concentrate on the beauty around her. The fields were gold with heavy-headed, ripened grain, and she could see, here and there, a few farmers walking slowly through the corn, verifying its ripeness.

When she got to the wood that bordered the Barrands' property and Ashford, she dismounted and led her mare along the narrow path. It was a relief to be in the shade, for the August sun was hot even before noon.

It wasn't long before she reached the famous tree where she had struggled and waited for her forgetful rescuer. She leaned her back against it and closed her eyes, and it seemed to her that nothing much had changed. Oh, she was older, and she was not really tied to the old oak. But she felt as trapped as she had then, this time by the bonds of love. Would it always be so, that a part of her, weeping and struggling, would wait for Tony to come and rescue her? Even if he did indeed marry another? What a pitiful woman she was were that true, she thought. She pulled herself away from the old tree and wished that Tony was in front of her, wished she could attack him again, kicking his shins or another part of his anatomy that was more vulnerable. Damn him, why couldn't he *see* her? Any why couldn't she stop loving him?

Tony had heard of Joanna's return and waited a day before calling on her. She was in the garden with her mother, the two of them in old smocks and carrying baskets for the seeds they were collecting from the lavender and marigolds. Tony took Lady Barrand's basket and followed them around, chatting about this and that while Joanna moved ahead of them, hardly acknowledging his presence. Finally, as they came to the end of the path, she stopped and said coolly, "I am surprised that you find the time to visit, Tony. Surely you are busy preparing for the harvest?"

"Most of it is done, thanks to my excellent manager," he said with a smile. "We expect to begin tomorrow or the next day, depending on the weather."

"Thomas said that too," said Lady Barrand. Looking up at the cloudless blue sky, she added, "And it looks as if the weather will hold."

"I hope so, my lady. I must be off, Joanna. It is good to see you home, looking so rested. Keswick seems to have agreed with you. You are quite the 'nut-brown maid!'"

Lady Barrand laughed. "Yes, she reminds me of my little girl Jo, who ran wild with you and Ned every summer."

Tony smiled, but Joanna, who finally let herself glance up at him, saw the pain in his eyes.

"I sometimes wish that we had one of those summers back, don't you, Jo?" he asked.

"There are times when I think things haven't changed at all," she replied, her voice even and noncommittal. "On a summer's day like today it is easy to think so."

Tony said his good-byes and after he left, Joanna gave a heavy sigh. "Sometimes I think *he* hasn't changed at all," she murmured.

"Oh, no, my dear," said her mother, putting her arm through Joanna's as they walked back to the house. "Tony has at last grown-up. Oh, he is not Ned, he never will be. But he doesn't need to be, does he? Tony Varden is turning out to be a fine Earl of Ashford in his own right."

"So it seems, Mother. And he will likely do his next duty as you and Father said, finding some willing young miss this next year," she said bitterly.

Lady Barrand stopped. "I think you are wrong, Joanna. I think things have changed. The seasons may turn and return, but you and Tony are *not* only old friends, although you are certainly that. You are two adults who have shared much: the loss of Ned and a harrowing ordeal this spring. One does not come through that unscathed."

"But Tony has never shown me any sign that he thinks of me romantically."

"And have you ever given him an occasion to think differently of you? Whenever I see the two of you together, you are the good old Jo, who keeps her feelings well hidden."

"I don't want to embarrass Tony, Mother. Nor awaken his pity."

"Well, my dear, if you would have his love, you may need to risk both! You know, Joanna," continued her mother, "there is something to be said for gambling. For risking all on the turn of a card, the roll of the dice. I think I understand why Tony was drawn into it after Ned died. When you risk all, you feel very much alive, and between the army and Ned he was so mired in death."

"Mother!"

"Oh, I am not saying that compulsive gaming is a *good* thing, Joanna. But neither is always keeping yourself safe."

The next day proved as fine as the last, and the harvest began. It was traditional for the gentlemen in the neighborhood to join their workers for a few hours of scything, and Tony welcomed the custom. He needed to lose himself in some repetitive activity so he would not think of Joanna. God knew what he would do with himself after the harvest. He might have to make a trip to London and Mrs. Spencer's.

The ladies of the neighborhood usually rode out with cider and bread and cheese for the harvesters. Lady Barrand had plenty of help from her servants, so Joanna decided to ride on to Ashford to see how their harvest was going.

Since Lady Ashford was not up to it, the housekeeper had organized the refreshments, and by the time Joanna arrived, the wagon was there and the men were just coming in from the fields. The smells of sweat, cider, ale, and ripened grain was a heady and familiar combination, and Joanna could have closed her eyes and imagined herself at any harvest over the last twenty years.

Tony was one of the last off the field. He was wearing an old pair of corduroys and a muslin shirt that was open almost to his waist. Joanna couldn't keep her eyes off the golden curls on his chest, which were darkened with sweat. Her eyes followed the line of hair down to where it disappeared beneath his pants. It was hard to bring her eyes back to his face and smile naturally at him.

"Come to help us, have you, Jo?" he teased her.

"I thought I'd see how the Ashford men were progressing, Tony." There had been a friendly but serious rivalry between the two estates over which brought in the harvest first, and the men around the wagon began to joke about how if the Barrand men had to send their lady to spy, they must be behind indeed.

"We are generous to losers, aren't we?" teased Tony as he handed Joanna a mug of cider. "Here, Jo. You can tell them we will be done well before sunset."

Their hands brushed as Joanna took the mug, and she shivered. She might have loved Tony for years and dreamed of kisses and perhaps more, but never had she been so aware of his masculinity as today. The cider was hard and strong, and after only a few sips she could feel it touch the base of her spine, warming her from there upward.

Tony's eyes blazed a bright blue out of his brown face. His hair had been bleached silver in places from his hours outdoors. His chest was getting red, and without thinking, Joanna reached out and touched him gently with her hand. "You had better be careful, Tony," she said. "You'll be blistered tonight."

As soon as she realized what she was doing, she pulled her hand back as though it had been burned, and blushed as red as his chest. Putting down her mug, she bade farewell to the crew, saying that she could tell the Barrand men to rest easy, since Ashford was now clearly a half hour behind!

"Don't listen to her," Tony said laughingly. "She says it only to worry us. Good-bye, my lady spy," he called, and Joanna waved as she rode off.

Tony went back to work, but somehow his aching muscles couldn't help him forget Joanna's light touch. Surely if it had been the thoughtless gesture of an old friend, she wouldn't have blushed like that.

38

The Barrands always held a supper dance after the final work of the harvest was done. Both Tony and Joanna were in a state of nervous anticipation for hours beforehand. Tony managed to spill sherry on his best breeches and then split a seam on the shoulder of his coat as he tried to squeeze his more muscular frame into it. His valet was almost in despair, but managed to dress him almost to satisfaction in his second-best outfit. Tony laughed and reminded him that at least now he *had* a second suit of clothes and hadn't had to sell them.

He set out late and arrived just before everyone was seated for supper.

Joanna had been equally at sixes and sevens, but had managed to dress without destroying any of her wardrobe. She was wearing the sea-foam green gown that she had worn in London, and Tony, who was seated across from her, couldn't keep his attention on his supper partner, the vicar's wife.

Tony claimed Joanna for two dances, a waltz and a cotillion. Their waltz lived up to neither's expectations. They were both aroused by their closeness to one another, yet were too unsure of each other to enjoy it. By the end of the dance, Joanna was convinced that Tony still felt nothing more for her than affection, and was about to give herself over to despair. But she remembered her mother's advice, and as they walked over to join a group of their neighbors, she managed to ask him if he would like to join her for an early-morning ride, now that the work of the harvest was done.

* * *

The next morning, she regretted her impulsiveness. She had spent her summer away from Kent in order to kill off the hope that he might one day look at her as a lover. She thought she had done it. She had returned home feeling calm and ready to turn her mind and heart to other possibilities. And the first time she saw him, bloody hope sprang eternal, she thought. Well, done was done, but this was the last time she would risk her heart, no matter what her mother's advice.

When Tony arrived, Joanna was waiting for him, and she hurried them off, not wanting to spend one second more than was necessary in that awful state of anticipation and despair that came over her in his presence.

It was a sunny day, but already there was a hint of autumn in the air, as if the weather knew the harvest was in, and it was safe for the cold to return.

They rode slowly along the boundary of the two properties and chatted about Tony's plans for Ashford.

"Lady Fairhaven proved a good and generous friend," said Joanna softly.

"Yes. She changed my life. And a few others," he added with a grin, "Jim, the erstwhile clerk and footman, is planning to purchase a tobacco shop. He has become his own man."

"But that is also thanks to you, Tony," Joanna reminded him.

"And Gideon Naylor . . ." Tony chuckled.

"What of Gideon?"

"He hardly presents himself as a romantic figure, does he?"

Joanna laughed. "Indeed not. He is much too ordinary-looking. And strong feeling is not something I would associate with him."

"Oh, but there is strength and passion there, Joanna. Remember, I saw him in action. Gideon plans to continue for a few more years as a Runner while Mrs. Blisse Spencer trains Carrie to take over her, uh, business and then the two of them will retire to Somerset."

"What was Mrs. Spencer's house like, Tony?" Joanna asked without thinking.

"A very clean, orderly, and well-disciplined establishment, I can assure you. But I should not be discussing bawdy houses with you, Joanna!"

"It is surely the only chance I would ever have to picture the inside of one. Do you think Mrs. Spencer worthy of Gideon?"

"Mrs. Spencer is Gideon's match in every way, I would think. And she hasn't been personally involved with customers for a number of years."

Joanna was curious about Tony's familiarity with whores and whorehouses, but even she was not bold enough to ask those questions.

They were now approaching what Joanna considered their wood and had to make a choice whether to go through the trees or around them.

"Why don't we visit the old oak today, Joanna?" Tony suggested.

Joanna nodded her agreement and they walked their horses down the small path that wound its way through the trees.

At a certain point it was easier and safer to dismount, and Tony slipped quickly off his horse in order to be there for Joanna. She had been ready to dismount by herself, and when his hands went around her waist to lift her off, she ended up falling against his chest.

Tony held her there for a minute, feeling the softness of her breasts under the light wool habit, and drank in the scent of lavender water that she was accustomed to wear. Joanna felt as if time had stopped, and then, all of a sudden, he let her down and turned away quickly.

He had to turn away to hide the evidence of his arousal. Thank God, ladies went first, he thought, as they led their horses. Or maybe not, he groaned to himself, catching glimpses of Joanna's curves as she moved gracefully in front of him. But by the time they reached the old oak, he had himself under control.

He wondered what she was thinking. Was she remembering all the make-believe that had brought her and Ned and him together? He could almost hear the faint echo of their voices in the wood. Ned was more present here than anywhere else, and Tony realized that finally he was at peace with his brother's loss. He would always miss him, always believe that Ned would have been the better earl, but he knew he could always come here and find him again.

"I *miss* Ned," said Joanna, turning around to look at Tony.

Tony took her reins and tied both horses to a nearby tree. He gestured to an old stump that had served as Joanna's throne, the Round Table, or anything else they required it to be, and she sat down. Tony leaned back against the oak and was silent for a minute. "I miss him too, but a moment ago I felt he was right here with us. I will never be able to replace him, but at last I feel I am not letting him down."

"I think," said Joanna slowly, "that you might well turn out to be better for Ashford."

Tony looked at her in surprise.

"Ned wasn't very interested in change, Tony. Or taking chances. He would have continued to run the estate the way your father had. And his father. You are a risk-taker, and in the long run, that may very well be what the Varden family needs in an earl!"

"Thank you, Jo. That means a great deal to me. Although I didn't think you much appreciated the risk-taker in me!"

"Not when you were merely wasting yourself at the tables, no."

"Or even when I was in the army."

"I confess that your propensity to rush into adventures, forgetting those you left behind, has caused me some concern, my lord!"

Tony laughed. "You will never forget that day I forgot I was Lancelot, will you? But I did eventually come to your rescue, Jo."

"By that time I had almost gotten myself free."

"Yes, and I still have the scars to prove it," said Tony, rubbing one leg against the other.

Joanna didn't smile at his joke, but sat there quietly, suddenly experiencing what felt like her whole history with Tony. She was the young Joanna, waiting patiently, then angrily, for her supposed champion. She was the Joanna of her first two Seasons, hoping against hope that when Tony was back on one of his infrequent leaves he would notice her. She was the Joanna of the past year, living daily with the expectation that he was to wed another woman. And here she was today, the whole come full circle. Her heart was too full of grief and anger to hold it in anymore. She had been "good old Jo" all these years so that at least she would have Tony's friendship, if nothing else. But at this moment, she didn't *care* whether she lost him as a friend or not. She looked up at him and said, with suppressed passion, "If I had the courage I had as a girl, I would be kicking your shins right now." Her voice was shaking and, to her horror, her eyes were filling up and overflowing.

"Why, Jo, what is it?" Tony was bending over her.

"Don't call me that!"

"Don't call you Jo? Why, Jo is my oldest and dearest friend," said Tony tenderly, kneeling down in front of her.

"Yes, and that is all she is. She is good old Jo; she doesn't mind waiting for me to remember that I am her knight. She'll always be there for the times when I think to come home. When I am not risking my life in Spain or my estate on St. James Street, or my heart with Lady Fairhaven. Well, I will not be good old Jo for you another minute, Tony Varden," said Joanna, pushing him away so hard that he landed on his rump, looking as startled and surprised as when she had attacked him years ago.

She laughed. She couldn't help it. Tony gave her a hesitant smile, which disappeared when he realized she had gone from laughter to tears in an instant.

"Joanna, dearest, don't cry like this." He was beside her

now, holding her against him. She tried to pull away, but he wouldn't let her. "Please listen to me for a minute."

He was smoothing her hair and gently rocking her, and her sobbing slowly subsided.

"Joanna, I have always loved to wager. My life against the French. Anything against the cards. And perhaps you are right, my life, not against Claudia so much as with Claudia against the odds. And a part of my heart was involved in that gamble, Joanna. But I would like to take one last risk. To lay one last wager on the table. All or nothing. My heart is yours, Jo, if you want it. I'm wagering that you do love me, that you do want me. I'm wagering that we could make a fine life together, Jo. And I *will* call you Jo, because she is who I loved first. Oh, I never knew how much a part of me she was. I took her quite for granted, I admit. But here I am at last, her knight most errant, hoping she will play this last gamble with me."

Joanna sat very still, her soul shivering at Tony's low-pitched voice. It was almost too much, after all these years, to be hearing what she had dreamed of hearing. She couldn't take it in at once and so she said nothing.

Tony waited, and then releasing her gently, stood up. "It is all right, Joanna. I understand that it is too late. Or that you can't trust that I would be worth the risk. And you will always have my friendship, whether you wish it or not."

It took Joanna another minute to understand what Tony was saying.

"I love you, Tony Varden. I have loved you since I was ten and I will love you until I die," she said fiercely.

Tony turned back to her, and then she was in his arms, crying and laughing again.

She pulled back after a moment and said: "Now I have put my heart on the table, and you haven't yet said you loved me."

He was about to protest, when she added, "Well, not in so many words."

He grasped her hand and led her over to the old oak, where they sat down, their backs to the broad trunk. Tony lifted her chin and looked directly into her eyes. "I love you, Jo. Joanna. Lady Joanna Barrand. Lady Ashford?" Joanna nodded and he leaned down to kiss her gently on the lips. Joanna opened her mouth under his soft pressure and welcomed him in a longer, deeper kiss.

They slipped down and were lying in each other's arms and Tony's hand reached in back to unbutton the top of her habit. He slipped inside and caressed one soft breast. Joanna gasped with delight and she moved her own hand to Tony's shirt. She twined her fingers in the blond curls on his chest, something she had been wanting to do since the day of the harvest. She could feel him stirring and swelling against her hips. She almost pulled away, but then lowered her hand to rest on this moving, living part of him that was fighting to get free.

Tony covered her hand with his and moved it back to his chest. "I do not want to take you on the forest floor, Jo. If you keep touching me, I will forget my resolve."

Joanna buried her head against his shoulder, flushed with both desire and embarrassment. "I am sorry, Tony."

"Sorry! Oh, no, Jo, don't be sorry. I want more than anything for you to touch me, but we will wait until you are my wife."

They had to get up, of course, or else nothing could have stopped them. They brushed the leaf mold off each other and when Joanna reached out to take a piece of oak leaf out of Tony's curls, he pulled her to him again for another long kiss.

"Come on, my dear," he said, finally pulling away. "This old wood has us under a spell."

"If this is what Guinevere felt for Lancelot, then I think I understand better why she betrayed her husband," Joanna confessed with a rueful smile.

"And I am glad that we only were playing at their story as children. Our story will have no such tragic ending, Jo."

"Ah, but it could have had so easily, Tony."

"Only because I was a fool. But I am no longer, Jo. I now appreciate what is valuable enough to wager my heart for."

AUTHOR'S NOTE

I am deeply indebted to the anonymous author of *The Fatal Effects of Gambling exemplified in the Murder of Mr. Weare and the Trial and Fate of John Thurtell* published by Thos. Kelly of Paternoster Row, London, in 1824. Without his detailed descriptions, I would not have been able to paint so authentically the inside of a gaming hell.

"Rouge et Noir," which was played nightly at most hells, bears a resemblance to our Blackjack. Court cards counted for ten, aces for one, and the rest of the cards as marked. The dealer always dealt the black first. As soon as the count went over thirty, he would call the final digit (i.e., "one" for thirty-one, "three" for thirty-three, etc.), stop, and then deal red. Whichever color was closest to thirty won. If both turned up thirty-one, the dealer called "one *après*" and dealt again.

The odds were, as always, against the gambler. As *Fatal Effects* tells us, a person playing every day and wagering only £1 per deal, was set to lose £5616 in a year. The hells took in about £500,000 per year despite the fact that gambling was illegal.